J. Margot Critch cur
Newfoundland, with h
two little buddies, Sim
amounts of time writin
music and looking out
trying to decide if she wants coffee or a margarita.

If you liked *Boardroom Sins*, why not try

Burn Me Once by Clare Connelly
Pleasure Games by Daire St. Denis
Legal Attraction by Lisa Childs

Discover more at millsandboon.co.uk

BOARDROOM SINS

J. MARGOT CRITCH

MILLS & BOON

All rights reserved including the right of reproduction
in whole or in part in any form. This edition is published
by arrangement with Harlequin Books S.A.

This is a work of fiction. Names, characters, places, locations
and incidents are purely fictional and bear no relationship to
any real life individuals, living or dead, or to any actual places,
business establishments, locations, events or incidents.
Any resemblance is entirely coincidental.

This book is sold subject to the condition that it shall not,
by way of trade or otherwise, be lent, resold, hired out
or otherwise circulated without the prior consent of the publisher
in any form of binding or cover other than that in which it is published
and without a similar condition including this condition
being imposed on the subsequent purchaser.

® and TM are trademarks owned and used by the trademark owner
and/or its licensee. Trademarks marked with ® are registered with the
United Kingdom Patent Office and/or the Office for Harmonisation
in the Internal Market and in other countries.

First Published in Great Britain 2018
by Mills & Boon, an imprint of HarperCollins*Publishers*
1 London Bridge Street, London, SE1 9GF

© 2018 Juanita Margot Critch

ISBN: 978-0-263-93217-1

MIX
Paper from
responsible sources
FSC C007454

This book is produced from independently certified FSC™ paper
to ensure responsible forest management.
For more information visit www.harpercollins.co.uk/green.

Printed and bound in Spain
by CPI, Barcelona

To my badass older sister, Claudette. Thank you for teaching me to know my worth, how to take no crap, and to live my life how I see fit. I know you've always loved me, even though I was SUCH A PEST, and you threatened to hang me up by my ankles more than once. I'm sorry I laughed when you said *The Purge* could happen. I think you might have been right. I love you, Sissy!

To Taryn Leigh Taylor, my Blaze Babe and Dare Darling. Thank you for the rant sessions and the encouragement. You're an amazing sounding board, colleague, confidant and friend. We got this!

To Johanna, Kathleen and the rest of the editorial team at Mills & Boon. This book was a challenge, and yet you all stood by me and helped me piece it together. Thank you for the support, guidance and patience. I couldn't do this without you. I'm blessed to have such wonderful, dedicated people on my team.

CHAPTER ONE

BRETT COLLINS WAS BORED.

He looked past his circle of friends as they talked among themselves, barely hearing what they were discussing, and he scanned the large room. He'd grown up in rooms like this, attending parties like this. As the only son of one of the most influential businessmen in Las Vegas, he'd gotten to know all the players at a young age. But as he sipped his glass of soda water, he almost sighed out loud. The same faces, the same discussions, the same deals.

He was restless. He wanted—*needed*—a challenge. Something new.

Collins/Fischer—the real estate development company he'd started with his friend Alex, the linchpin of their other operations—had seen great success in the past years, and they'd maintained a comfortable spot near the top. But he wanted more. He wanted to be number one. And as he looked across the room for inspiration, a sign of what would be next for him, he found nothing.

Inherently, Brett hated schmoozing parties, preferring instead to meet with people in a less manufactured setting. But they did serve their purpose: talking to people, finding out the local gossip—who had been fired, who had been hired, who'd signed what deals, who was under indictment, who was sleeping with whom. And that was why he and The Brotherhood—his closest friends and business partners since college—had gone to Mayor Thompson's party. To look for their next opportunity to strike, to make another splash on the local scene. At only thirty, they'd all done quite well for themselves, and while many in the room hated and feared them, were jealous of and intimidated by the business acumen of the group, they all still wanted a piece of them. Everyone in the room would benefit from a close relationship with the members of The Brotherhood.

There was Alex, his business partner in real estate; Gabe, one of the top lawyers in the city; Rafael, a Las Vegas city councillor; and Alana, the only woman in their circle, who was a talented interior designer, but she'd become the manager of the group's restaurants and exclusive club. Together they made up The Brotherhood—and together they planned to use their expertise and influence to run the city.

Needless to say, they weren't at the party for social purposes. They'd secured for themselves a quiet corner of the room, near the bar, to establish their game plan for the evening. Whom they each needed to talk to, what they hoped to accomplish and just when the hell they could get out of there. But Brett couldn't manage to focus his tired mind. He'd had a rough couple of weeks, workwise, and it was all thanks to Rebecca Daniels, the devastatingly sexy CEO of Daniels International, a rival real estate development firm. She was a major threat currently, but he and Rebecca also had a fiery past.

Brett turned back to his friends and took another drink from his glass. The soda water, infused with lime and basil, was refreshing but didn't improve his mood. His friends were listing the important people they wanted to approach and make connections with, but Brett could find no one in attendance whom he was interested in seeing. He couldn't deal with another stuffed shirt or old cohort of his father's coming up to him and asking about the elder Collins, instead of expressing interest in Brett's endeavors. Brett loved and respected his father, but even in his years of running his own successful empire, he'd found it difficult to blaze his own trail in the shadow of Garrett Collins, one of the city's most influential men.

"Did you see that the Heinrich brothers are here tonight?" Alana asked the group, gesturing to two men in the center of the room. "I might have to go introduce myself. They're visiting from Sweden, looking to open a new hotel on the Strip, and I heard they may be looking for a design collaborator," she said, turning on her most seductive smile, sauntering away and raising her hand in greeting.

"And Mayor Thompson is finally free," Rafael said. "I'd better go put in an appearance, seeing as I'm trying to secure his endorsement before I announce I'm running for mayor." He stepped away, as well.

Alex leaned in. "Brett, the guy from Permits is here and we need to talk to him. See if we can't grease the wheels and get the paperwork quickly approved for the new subdivision."

Brett nodded without much interest.

Alex didn't miss it. "Everything okay?"

"Yeah. I'm just tired, I guess. I haven't slept much this week. This messing around with Daniels International is starting to get to me." It all started a few months ago when the other company had outmaneuvered Brett and Alex in scooping up and securing a huge deal out from under them, costing Collins/Fischer a small fortune. Brett and Alex had responded by buying out one of Daniels's key suppliers and raising the prices. He could only imagine the scrambling that had gone on at DI that day. But then Rebecca had countered by poaching one of their VPs and giving him a place at Daniels International. Escalation had been quick, vicious, and he'd racked his brain trying to figure out his next step. But it had to be big. Nobody screwed with Collins/Fischer. Brett had to end the feud, and quick.

"You have to put it aside," Alex told him. "We shouldn't let this escalate too much. We need to focus on our own work and not worry about Rebecca Daniels or Daniels International." Brett opened his mouth to speak, but Alex plowed over him. "I know you guys have history. But focus. What's important now is our own success, not revenge."

"Whatever history I may or may not have with Rebecca Daniels has nothing to do with the business."

"You've been working day and night for the past couple of months. Why don't you go on home? Get some sleep, go to the club and get laid, watch TV, whatever. I can handle things here. I'll talk to the permits guy."

Sex and sleep—hell, even crashing in front of the television—definitely sounded better than smooth talking anyone in attendance at the party, but he couldn't make himself leave and take a night off. If he wasn't working, or thinking about work, it felt like he was wasting his time. Work provided the necessary distraction from his thoughts and darker urges. "I know you can handle it. But you know me. I don't do well with downtime," Brett returned, grimacing. Downtime led to boredom, and boredom led to cravings. He sipped his water again.

"Yeah, but it isn't healthy to spend every waking moment thinking about the business."

"Are you really giving me this lecture? You're just like me."

Alex laughed, and Brett followed his friend's gaze across the room, until it landed on a gorgeous blonde wearing a tight black dress. "Yeah, but I know how to take the night off to allow time for the finer things." The blonde looked back and smiled, waving to Alex. "And that's my cue," he muttered and sauntered away to focus on the *finer things*, leaving Brett alone.

Brett knocked back the rest of his water and put his glass on the bar. Maybe he should leave, see what he could get up to at Di Terrestres. He scanned the crowd one more time, hoping to find inspiration for the next big project, the one that would make him and his friends, The Sin City Brotherhood, legends of Las Vegas. He watched the door to the ballroom open, and a beautiful, glamorous woman entered the party. And his eyes connected with the one face that made his blood boil with anger and lust—the blast from the past who was currently working tirelessly to ruin his life. The woman who plucked his memories, tore at his chest and stiffened his posture, not to mention his dick—Rebecca Daniels.

Rebecca smoothed a hand down the front of her black silk dress and straightened the hem that hit several inches above her knees. She accepted a glass of champagne from a server balancing a tray on his fingertips, and she sipped from it. She'd been attending events like Mayor Thompson's party for years, and they were like second nature to her. She felt at ease, able to mingle her way through the crowds, shift in and out of conversations. But that night, she wanted no more than to go home and crash in her bed. She'd had a long few weeks—an even longer few months since her father had passed away six months ago and she'd taken the helm of Daniels International. She'd had time for little else than work lately.

Her father had excelled at functions like this; he'd made time for everyone and had had the ability to make everyone he interacted with feel like the most important person in the room, even when he was exhausted and overworked. And so could she. It was something he'd passed on to Rebecca, but though she was good at networking, her father had been legendary.

She sipped her champagne again, willing the alcohol to whisk away the melancholy. But it wasn't working. Frowning, she realized that she shouldn't have even come here, and she wouldn't have if she hadn't been personally invited by Mayor Thompson, who was a close family friend.

"My God, Rebecca." She heard a pleasant greeting from her right. She turned and saw Ben Thompson, the city's long-standing mayor, and his wife, Esther, coming toward her. She smiled as they each embraced her.

"How are you, dear?" Ben asked her. "I'm sorry we haven't been in touch since the funeral. Your father is truly missed."

"Thank you. I miss him, too."

"Thank you for coming tonight," Ben said, patting her hand with his. "I'm glad you were able to make it."

Rebecca smiled, knowing that he meant it. She'd always had such great memories of Ben and Esther, of family barbecues and vacations. After Rebecca's mother passed away when she was a baby, Esther had stepped in to be a sort of surrogate, providing love, support and guidance; and Ben had always been at her father's side, avuncular, an uncle figure since her childhood.

"I wouldn't have missed it for the world, and I'm well," she said. "How are you both?"

"Things are good," Ben answered. "I'm retiring this year and finally stepping down. I don't think I have another campaign in me."

"Oh, really?" Rebecca was surprised to hear it. "And then what will you do with your time?"

"I'm going to make him relax," Esther answered. "Days filled with golf, traveling, arts and crafts—"

"Sounds awful," Ben interrupted, and they all laughed. "Dear," he said as he reached out for her hand, "we must move on, but let's get together sometime soon."

"Absolutely." Rebecca smiled as the couple left to greet another set of guests.

Satisfied with her first social interaction of the evening, Rebecca took a deep breath and scanned the room. Sipping her champagne again, she felt her confidence bolster. Despite the size of her father's enormous shoes, and how hard she'd been working to fill them, she knew she could do this. She could handle being the new face and CEO of Daniels International. This job was in her blood.

Rebecca's gaze struck on one of the reasons for her increased workload. Brett Collins was arrogant, stubborn and probably looking for retribution after the recent series of events between their two companies.

But that didn't mean she couldn't be physically affected by him.

Every system in her body ran hot as she saw him casually lean an elbow against the bar. He was alone, but it didn't seem to bother him as he lounged confidently like a king—or a god among men. His eyes roamed over the crowd, sharp and methodical as he scanned the room, until they connected with hers.

At that moment, time stopped for Rebecca as the rest of the room—the party, the revelers, the music—fell away. Her breath halted as he held her stare, transfixed, unable to turn away even if she wanted to. Just like what happened every time she faced him, she got lust-inspired tunnel vision. They had history, and she was brought back to her under-grad days in college. The thing between her and Brett had always been hot, heavy, intense. Since day one of freshman year in college, they'd butted heads, and now they were entangled in a rivalry between their firms—two of the biggest in Las Vegas—and eventually only one would survive.

Rebecca saw Brett's eyes narrow, and he straightened to full height. His body was still similar to the one she'd known so intimately before as a younger woman, but in the past few years, she was pleased to see that he was even larger, stronger—a more grown version of her old enemy and lover. His broad shoulders and strong back were clad in the fine dark blue material of an immaculately tailored suit. Along with his dark blond hair and blue eyes, he still possessed Adonis-like traits—a strong jaw, straight nose and high cheekbones. But, she noticed, the deep dimples that she remembered at the edges of a youthful, cocky smile were absent these days, seemingly unable to coexist with the cold, hard stare of Brett Collins, the real estate mogul.

His gaze didn't waver from her, and she returned his stare, matching the intensity, or at least trying to. Brett's attention was powerful. He might have been compelling in his twenties. But at thirty the man was downright potent.

He smiled at her, looking just as arrogant and smug as ever. The deep breath she took to steady herself shuddered out of her as she exhaled. Even after five years, the pull of him was still as strong as a team of horses.

Everyone moved about them, oblivious to the tension that traveled across the room between her and Brett. Shaking her head, she forced herself to pull it together. Rebecca was a strong, grown woman who had made multimillion-dollar deals and stared down some of the top businessmen and women from Vegas to New York City. If she was going to be living in the same city as Brett, she was bound to run into him again. What could it hurt to talk to her former lover? She had to get it over with, and when she did, she could forget about him and get on with her life. So straightening her posture and flipping her hair behind her shoulders, she strode confidently in the direction of Brett Collins.

Brett watched Rebecca as she crossed the floor toward him, trying to hide the smile that made the corners of his lips creep upward. She'd come back from New York after five years on the East Coast and had landed squarely back on Brett's radar. Despite that they had their own long-standing rivalry, he'd been competing with her father, Hiram, in the local real estate industry for years, and the feud had continued when Rebecca took over. They'd been at each other's throat for months, but this was the first time he'd seen her in person since she'd returned to town, and it was affecting him more than he liked.

He'd spent college neck and neck with her, competing for grades, awards, accolades, top position in the class. By coincidence, they'd earned undergraduate and graduate degrees from the same schools, so that meant that they couldn't escape one another. And from day one, they had not clicked. He was confident, maybe a bit cocky; she was stubborn and not willing to relent, and neither of them knew what to do with the other. They'd had a frustrating, competitive, downright antagonistic back-and-forth relationship—well, if you would call their *enemies with benefits* hookups a relationship. They would fight, then fuck, then go back to fighting…for *six years*.

They'd had major chemistry, and she was still somehow even more infuriatingly sexy than she'd been all those years ago. So maybe he had some memories of the past rumbling below his belt, but there was no reason for his reaction to her now, the pounding in his chest or the way the blood rushed past his ears, heading south, causing a stirring in his dick as she came closer. That was unexpected. He put down his glass and fisted his hands at his sides to hide their shaking, frustrated and unsure if the tremors came from anger or lust.

She moved, almost gliding across the floor in her stiletto heels. The sheen of her black dress caught his attention, reflecting light as it clung to her curves. No doubt, she was still the gorgeous, sexy, glamorous woman she'd always been, but there was something else. She was confident, owning the room, tossing her blond hair behind her shoulders and catching the eyes of men and women as she approached. Outside of sex, they'd never seen eye to eye, no matter how stunning she was or how sexually compatible they'd been. But as she got closer to him with every step, his breaths became shorter and his eyes narrowed further. He tried to act cool, but the line that he could feel forming between his eyebrows betrayed him.

"Hi, Brett," she said, a smile playing on her red lips. Brett knew people, and while she appeared confident, he wondered if underneath her calm exterior she was trying to rein in her emotions. Just like he was.

"Becca Daniels." He smirked, calling her the name she'd used when she was younger.

"Rebecca," she corrected him with a smile.

"Right," he said, flashing a small smile at her correction. "Sorry. *Rebecca Daniels*." He could feel himself becoming rigid, and yet more aroused, as if his body was unsure how to react to her presence. He didn't know whether he should scream at her, walk away or lift her onto the nearby table and fuck her in the middle of the party. But civility won out and he extended his hand to her for a polite shake. She smiled and took his hand. They shook hands. "It's been a while since we've been in the same room."

He nodded. "It has been."

"That hasn't stopped us from doing business, though."

"Doing business?" he asked with a snide smile. "Is that what you call what we've been doing? Poaching one of my executives? I'll have you know that the minute I get word he's violated his non-disclosure agreement, you'll be hearing from our lawyers."

"I'll have you know that none of us want to know your illicit secrets. We aren't interested. But while we're on the topic, what about our lumber supplier for our latest development? I believe it now falls under the umbrella of Collins/Fischer. Charging outrageous prices. How many contractors did you leave scrambling with those changes you made?"

Brett snorted. They'd changed the terms only on the DI contract. "I assure you, that was a coincidence," he lied.

She rolled her eyes, rightfully not believing him. "You just did it because you were pissed that we outbid you on the sale of that factory in Reno. Am I right?"

"I guess we'll never know." Brett shrugged. That was the exact event that had started the series of events that had led them to this conversation. He and Alex had been working to acquire an abandoned factory and warehouse in Reno to turn it into a high-end condo development. But at the eleventh hour, Daniels International had swooped in and taken it.

He looked over her shoulder and quickly saw his friends in the middle of their own conversations, but all their eyes were trained on him and his interaction with Rebecca. Ignoring them, Brett gave Rebecca all his attention. He plucked a champagne flute from the tray of a passing waiter and handed it to her. "We can rehash this all night, but let's talk. How does it feel to be back in town?"

Rebecca sipped from the glass and eyed him suspiciously over the rim. "It was a little strange at first. It was a challenge, but the transition to CEO has been smooth."

"Seriously, though, I was sorry to hear about your father. He was a good man."

"Thank you." She sipped her champagne again, her eyes not breaking contact with his. He couldn't remember the last time someone had so fully captured his attention. His eyes dropped to her mouth and the drop of champagne that clung to her top lip when she lowered her glass, and he somehow resisted the urge to lean in and sweep it up with his tongue.

Distracted by his desire, Brett barely heard the words she was saying as he looked her up and down. He could see the near-imperceptible changes in her demeanor, like the way she straightened under his scrutiny, the way her pupils dilated slightly as she spoke to him and the way her lips parted as she swiped her tongue over them. He grinned at her. Brett knew women, and Rebecca didn't have to say the words out loud. Her body language told him everything that he needed to know—she wanted him, too. Maybe as much as he wanted her—to once again bury himself deep inside her, momentarily revisiting the heat and passion they'd experienced before.

He stepped closer to her, touching his fingertips to the swell of her hip before spreading his hand over her, cupping her waist. "You know, I don't want to talk business. Why don't we go outside?" he asked, his voice lowered. He tilted his head in the direction of the door leading to the terrace. "We can *really* catch up."

She paused for a moment, hesitating, and he thought she would refuse—because, really, what could they possibly have to catch up on? But instead, she nodded. "Sure."

He slid his hand to her lower back, just above the rise of her ass, and escorted her through the double doors that led to the terrace, and he was pleased and surprised to find that they were alone out there. They walked to a far corner, and she leaned on the concrete railing, looking out at the view afforded by the mayor's mansion. He stood next to her and leaned on the railing, as well. He turned his head and watched her. Whatever was going on in Rebecca's mind made her eyebrows furrow. Maybe it matched his own turmoil, but he was confident that he could move past it. *But can she?*

She was quiet for a moment before she spoke. "I really missed it here." Her whisper was wistful and vulnerable. And the moment felt more real than any he ever remembered them sharing. Well, most of them. There had been the one or two nights in college when they'd almost hit on something more… He watched her as she looked across the desert to the lights of the city. They both knew the mountains were just on the horizon, completely obscured by the darkness. "New York was nice, bustling, and winter was kind of fun for the first few years. But for a city that claims to never sleep, it doesn't have quite the same insomnia as Vegas."

Brett moved closer to her. "Maybe Vegas missed you, too," he said, looking out at the horizon. "There's nowhere else in the world like this. Las Vegans can't expect to just settle anywhere else. There's something about the desert, the energy, just trying to survive in such a harsh landscape…" He trailed off and she turned her head and looked at him. They were again quiet in the moment they'd created. They were again, for a short time, just kids in their twenties, with their lives ahead of them, constantly at odds with each other but managing to somehow find some moments of levity that book-ended hot sex, before they went back to hating each other. Before starting the cycle over again. Rebecca always gave as good as she got and, standing next to her now, Brett realized that no matter what had happened between them or how crazy they made each other, he'd missed that about her.

Rebecca shook her head, breaking them from the moment. "So, what do you want to talk about?" she asked, not looking at him but still facing the darkened horizon, her arms folded in front of her on the stone partition that separated the rest of the mayor's garden.

"I lied. I don't really want to talk," he told her, shifting closer to her, and their arms touched. Through his suit jacket, he could feel her heat.

Her laugh was humorless. "Just perfect." She shook her head. "I should have known. I didn't come out here for a quick hookup, you know."

"Well, if you don't want to hook up, what is it *you* want to talk about?"

"I don't think I'm quite done talking about business."

Surprise drew Brett's head back. "Oh, really?"

She faced him full on—not many people stared him down like she was doing. "Yeah, you and I have had some dealings recently."

"Yeah. Just a bit of fun back and forth."

"Well, it's over. Starting right now."

"Oh, really?"

"Yeah, I'm running DI now, and I can tell you that I have a lot on my plate now and zero time for all the dick-measuring power struggles that have been going on between our two companies. I've got more important things to concentrate on than you. Let's just agree to end this now. Let me run my company, and you can run yours."

If Brett hadn't been so stunned, he would have thrown back his head in laughter. He couldn't remember the last time anyone had spoken to him like that. No, he could. It was definitely more than five years ago, in his last interactions with Rebecca. She might think they were done. But he wasn't done with her. Not by a long shot.

Even though he had plans for her businesswise, that would come tomorrow. He still had to contend with the rush of desire that tore through him, ratcheting up his heartbeat and hardening his cock. "That's probably enough about business," he said, his voice lowered, as he turned to face her. "Are you here alone tonight?" He looked back to the door that led inside. They were still the only people on the terrace. Nobody through that open door paid them any mind as the gentle notes of music were carried outside on the air.

"It's a little late for that question, isn't it?"

Brett grinned. It really didn't matter to him if she'd attended the party with another man or even if she was seeing anyone. He could tell that he had her. He inched closer and felt a surge of triumph when she didn't move away. It would be so easy to pull her into his embrace, to hold her, kiss her, just like old times. He wanted to feel her skin against his lips, under his fingers. He wanted no more than to be buried deeply inside her, fucking her until she clawed his back and screamed out his name... Shit, he needed to pull it together. He had more to consider here than just sex. Even if he did seduce her tonight, he had to keep a clear head or risk losing everything. And Brett didn't lose. Ever.

"Well, I just want to know that your attention is focused solely on me and not anyone else," he murmured, leaning even closer.

"And you're wondering if I have a boyfriend?"

He shook his head. "If you did have a boyfriend, I know you wouldn't be out here with me." He grinned again. "And even if you did, you wouldn't remember him after tonight anyway."

Rebecca blinked quickly, before she guffawed loudly, putting a palm on his chest to push him away. "You are so full of it." Incredulity made way for wanting as she involuntarily curled her fingers over the well-formed muscles of his chest. He might be wearing several layers of clothing between their skin touching, but she knew that he certainly didn't skimp on the workouts. He smiled at her, knowing. His straight white teeth and the devilish glint in his eye made her fingers twitch, eager to keep exploring, but she pulled back.

Years in corporate America had taught Rebecca how to keep her cool in high-pressure situations with important men and women, but Brett shook her. Sure, she put on a good show, trying to seem unaffected, but she'd seriously underestimated the impact of Brett Collins in the flesh. Everything about him, his essence, his energy, surrounded her completely. He was standing too close, and she could feel him, smell him, almost taste him. The spicy scent of his cologne was intoxicating. She looked back at the city skyline, taking a deep, cleansing breath to steady herself. It didn't work, and she cautioned a look at him. He was still leaning his elbow on the railing, facing her, watching her. His mood was impossible to read.

"I'm not here with anyone," she assured him.

"Good."

"How about you?" she asked, nodding in the

direction of the party. "Any of those pretty young things in there belong on your arm?"

He shrugged coolly. "With the exception of some women I see casually, I'm officially unattached. If there was time to build a relationship, I haven't found anyone I would want to do it with." She nodded. There was no doubt that he fooled around with women, a man like Brett, but it didn't matter. She had no ownership over him or whatever he did with his dick.

Slowly, Rebecca looked Brett up and down, his body hard and lean under his tailored suit. Her mind raced, and she cursed her hormones as she lost the ability to focus on anything but the unbridled memories she held of him. Her skin flushed, she could feel the slow rise of heat as it spread from her chest to her cheeks, and she blinked rapidly, clearing the erotic snapshots that flashed behind her eyes. She looked away from him briefly, and when she glanced back, he was watching her with a heated expression that told her he knew what she'd been thinking and was possibly running through his own slideshow of memories.

They grew quiet as they watched each other. Just looking at the man made Rebecca want to do awful, naughty, irresponsible things, despite her better judgment, and for just a moment, she let herself simply enjoy being in his company. Her guard just momentarily lowered. Her heart fluttered in her chest, unsteady. And despite every part of her mind, her heart, that told her to stay away, she stepped closer, bringing the tips of her breasts near enough to graze his chest. The movement sent a sizzle of electricity throughout her body, and she jumped back a little in reaction. He must have noticed it, too, because when she looked up at him, his eyes were narrowed, and one side of his mouth ticked upward in a seductive, lopsided grin. Without saying anything, he reached out and grasped both of her hips with his large hands, drawing her near.

"Brett," she whispered, her breath hitched in her throat. She ignored rational thought as her desire and nerve endings screamed at her to acquiesce, and she finally listened to what her body was saying, leaning into him. Before she knew it, she'd raised her face upward, just inches from his.

"Yeah?" He moved closer, his large hands spreading over the small of her back, and at a torturously slow speed, they moved lower and lower, causing a gasp to escape her parted lips.

"Don't," she pleaded, half-hearted, as he squeezed her ass, his fingers digging into her flesh. She tried to push him away, but every part of her body craved the attention of those fingers.

"Don't what?" he whispered. One hand released her behind and then took her hand. He brought her wrist to his lips, kissing her sensitized skin. She didn't answer. She couldn't. The words wouldn't form in her brain. "Don't what?" he asked, prodding before extending his tongue, dragging it over the electrified nerve endings of her inner arm.

Rebecca closed her eyes in surrender, unable to fight him. "Don't stop."

CHAPTER TWO

REBECCA'S WHISPERED PLEA was all Brett needed.

In one corner of his mind, he knew that they were still in public, but he was only faintly tuned in to the sounds of the party over his pounding heart and her shuddered breaths. Even though they were alone on the terrace, he knew that at any moment anyone could come join them outside and catch whatever moment he and Rebecca were caught in.

But it didn't matter to him, and he leaned forward and brushed his lips against hers. It was a soft touch at first, his lips just grazed against hers, but it wasn't enough. He went back for more. Her lips parted under his, and he brought his hands to her face, cupping her, holding her to him. It had been years since he'd last kissed her, but everything about it was familiar.

Her taste and the way she felt underneath his hands and lips felt right, and despite that, his brain pleaded with his body to remember that she was still the same woman who'd fought him tooth and nail these past months, used underhanded tricks to win five years before in grad school. But that didn't concern him now. Because she felt too god-damn good.

Rebecca whimpered into his mouth and tilted her head to the side, angling herself so that he could deepen the kiss. And he did. His tongue delved into her mouth and found hers, stroking, driving against one another. She raised her arms and wrapped them around his neck, drawing him closer. His cock thickened, and he felt it grinding painfully against the zipper of his pants. He had to use every ounce of his control to not yank them down and take her against the wall.

But he didn't pull away.

Instead he lowered his hand, releasing the grip he'd held on her gorgeous ass, and skimmed his palm down her outer thigh. He clutched her leg and raised it until she wrapped it around him. The skirt of her dress wasn't tight, and the looser material allowed him access to the smooth skin of her inner thigh as he let his hands drift upward toward the hem of her skirt. Soon, his fingers were underneath, fingering the lace of her panties.

"Brett, we can't do this here," she breathed. Those might have been her words, but she leaned into him, grasping his forearm, pulling him closer, thrusting desperately against his hand.

"Why not?" he growled.

"We're in public," she said. "As if that would stop you," she whispered with a sly grin.

"As if it would stop either of us," he agreed. "You never shied away from the risk of being caught before," he reminded her with a cocked eyebrow. Rebecca had had quite the exhibitionist streak, and he wondered if she still did.

Her gasp was his answer and reward when he pushed her panties aside and touched the bare lips of her pussy. Her legs parted farther, obediently, and his fingers delved between her wet folds, circling her clit several times.

Rebecca inhaled sharply as her head rolled back and her eyes drifted shut. Brett kissed her lips to silence her, blocking her body with his own, to keep her from the eyes of anyone who might come onto the terrace. Grasping her thigh, he pulled it higher, holding her so that she was open to him. Her eyes widened and found his when he thrust a finger inside her, and he relished the lustful sounds that emanated from her throat. With two fingers moving in and out of her, the heel of his hand made contact with her clit with every thrust. From the way her body quivered before him, he knew that she was just hanging on to the edge. He kept a steady pace, and when she tightened and clenched her muscles around him, she cried out into his mouth.

When she quieted, he pulled his mouth away

but drew her closer to him. "You always look so beautiful when you come," he whispered against her ear. "Your breath is shallow, your cheeks are flushed and your pupils are so dilated, I can barely see how beautifully blue they are." Where the hell had that come from?

She sighed, and he released his hold on her leg, letting her foot drop back to the floor. "Oh, my God, Brett." She sighed.

"Let's get out of here." Fingering her on a terrace during a party hosted by the mayor was one thing, but there was still so much more he wanted to do with Rebecca Daniels, *to her.* "We can go back to my place," he suggested hopefully, his lips just a whisper away from hers. He pressed them together for a second. Kissing her felt too damn good.

"I don't think that's a good idea," she told him.

"It definitely isn't." He grinned. "But let's do it anyway."

Rebecca's laugh was more heavy exhalation than humor, and he watched the storm as it progressed over her blue eyes. They had darkened significantly with desire, and the flush that colored her cheeks and her chest showed him that she was just as affected as he was. They heard laughter from the doorway leading into the house. Brett looked over his shoulder and saw that two men and a woman had just joined them outside. The trio barely gave them a second glance.

"I should go," she said, finding her own footing without his support. He pulled the front of his jacket over the bulge of his cock, disappointed, but he noted with satisfaction her wobbly stance. She turned away from him.

"Wait," he called.

"Yeah?"

He withdrew his wallet from the inside pocket of his jacket and took out a card. "Here," he said. "Take this."

"What is it?"

"If we're done talking business, come by some night."

"Di Terrestres?"

"Yeah, it's my club. The address is on there, and my cell number is on the back. I'll show you around. Soon."

Her lips twitched as she looked down at the card. She said nothing before she slid it into the pocket of her dress, and she walked away from him.

"It was nice seeing you, Becca," he called to her.

She stopped and turned. "Rebecca," she corrected him. "And you, too, Brett," she said, turning and walking away from him. "But don't forget. Don't come after DI anymore. I don't have time for games."

Brett took a deep breath and watched her walk away. He hadn't meant for any of that to happen. But he hadn't been able to control himself. He'd completely lost his mind. Apparently, all he had to do to forget business and their previous hostility was touch her and he became that same twenty-two-year-old who'd been hopelessly infatuated with her. His only hope was that she was just as shaken as he was…

He was going to have to learn to control himself if he was going to be anywhere near Rebecca Daniels again. How could he hook up with her on Saturday and go into work Monday clearheaded enough to deal with the fact he had to replace an executive VP thanks to her?

No. This would never do. He had to act now.

When Rebecca was completely out of sight, he nodded in recognition to the people who'd joined them on the terrace and headed back inside to the party. He saw his friends, who'd again found each other and taken their place in a small exclusive huddle near the bar. Alex, Rafael, Gabe and Alana watched him approach. They said nothing, but their raised eyebrows spoke volumes even as they each, almost simultaneously, raised their glasses to their lips to hide their smirks. He ordered another soda water from the bar and turned back to them.

"What?" he asked them.

They all played clueless for a moment, not answering until Alex finally broke. "Okay, what the hell was that?"

Brett shrugged. "What was what?"

Alex rolled his eyes. "Don't play stupid with us. What were you doing with Rebecca Daniels?"

"Nothing. We were talking. Just catching up."

"Just catching up with her tongue down your throat?" Alana countered.

"What did you see?" Brett narrowed his eyes.

Alana's widened. "What did you do?"

Brett took in the amused but concerned faces of his friends. "It was nothing. But something came to me. I've got an idea." He turned to Alex. "You know how we were talking about taking Collins/ Fischer to the next level?"

Alex eyed him, his stance wary. "Yeah, what do you have in mind?"

"We're going to be number one. And we're going to do that by dismantling the competition."

"Okay... How?"

"A takeover. I want us to buy out Daniels International." He let it sink in, aware of the curious and cautious way his friends eyed him.

"What?" Alex asked him.

"What aren't you getting here? They're a real estate development firm," Brett said. "So is Collins/ Fischer. We'll initiate a takeover. Buy them out. When we're successful in taking them out, we'll move on to the next one, then the next one, until we're the only game in town."

None of his friends looked convinced. They were silent until Alana spoke up first. "Why?" she asked.

He thought about his answer. He'd been looking for a project, the next business move. He'd always been in this for the long game—to be the only real estate firm in town. He'd been at battle with Daniels International for months, and the company's profits had been declining for years, partly because of stiff competition from Collins/Fischer. Why not start there? It was a logical procession. But he would be lying if he didn't admit that there was more to it. His lips pulled downward in a frown, and he let the flames of animosity fuel him. "Now's the time," he started. "We're on the verge of being on top of this city. And isn't that what we want? Our goal has always been to run this bitch," he reminded them. "A buyout. We'll get as many shares as we can." He looked at Gabe, an equal business partner in The Brotherhood's operations but also the group's lawyer. "Think we can get the paperwork by Monday morning?"

Brett hadn't even finished his sentence before Gabe had his phone in his hands, most likely writing a message to his assistant to start the work. "By 9:00 a.m.," he promised before looking up.

Alex also had his phone out, clearly engaged in getting a takeover bid in order for Monday. He and Alex had worked together, known each other long enough to trust each other fully. All Alex needed was to know Brett thought it was a good idea, a good move for the business, and he was on board. Only Alana eyed him skeptically.

"What?" he asked her.

"What's going on with you?"

"Nothing. We're just planning what's next for the businesses."

"But it's Rebecca," Alana reminded him. "She was my friend in college, and I spent as much time with her as I did you. You guys have this weird history. I know how you are together."

"How we *were* together," Brett corrected. "And Rebecca was nothing more than a hookup." When she eyed him skeptically, he amended his statement. "A hookup *nemesis*?"

"Who is this person?" Gabe asked, putting his phone back in his pocket. He hadn't gone to the same college as they had, having attended Harvard Law, and he hadn't heard the story. "Old girlfriend?"

"No," Brett said, definitive.

"She was in our undergrad and MBA programs," Alana explained. "She's so smart and just as stubborn as Brett, so you know they zeroed in on each other. They rivaled each other to be top of the class in every course. They competed for the best grades and for awards, but despite all the fighting and scornful looks, they hooked up all the time. I don't quite know how it happened, though."

Brett sighed. He knew that Alana and Rebecca had been friends, but he didn't realize that she'd been privy to all of the dirty details. Well, not all of them, apparently—she didn't know how it'd all started. One late night in the library before finals, they'd fought over the last private study room in the business library. But the fight hadn't lasted long before they'd agreed to share it. It had been only a matter of time before he had her lying on the small table of a study room, with his palm over her mouth to keep her from screaming out into the silence of the library, visible to anyone who walked by through the small window in the door.

From then on, they'd still challenged each other, in class and outside, but they couldn't stop themselves from giving in to their desires and enjoying private moments in public and semipublic spaces around campus. And that had gone on throughout their MBA program until she'd gone off to New York. "It doesn't matter how it happened."

"Okay, then how is she going to react when she sees the takeover bid on her desk on Monday morning?" Alana asked.

Brett didn't want to admit to his friends how much seeing her again had affected him, and how much his own reaction had surprised him. He had to fight the discombobulation that had come from being near her tonight, and even though he could still smell her on his fingers, taste her kiss on his lips, he'd immediately shifted back into business mode. Survival mode. When it came to work, he could overcome any feelings to focus on the business. He'd done it before, and he was goddamn sure he could do it again.

But he smiled, trying to appear more confident in his resolve than he felt. "It doesn't matter how she reacts," he told her. "It's business."

CHAPTER THREE

Y<small>AWNING</small>, R<small>EBECCA</small> <small>SAT</small> back in her father's—no, *her*—chair, and picked up the take-out paper cup that had contained four full shots of espresso only ten minutes ago. She'd taken a sip. It hadn't been enough. She'd needed more, and she gulped it down, completely draining the cup. The fear that she may need to go back to the lobby café was real. The coffee had done nothing to keep her awake, and she didn't think there was any amount of caffeine or makeup that would make her look or feel like a human being this morning. She hadn't slept in two nights, not since Mayor Thompson's party, and it was all Brett Collins's fault.

With a sigh, she dramatically threw her head back and swiveled around in her chair to face the back wall as she remembered how it felt to have him kiss her, touch her again. She'd gone five years not being with him. And she thought she'd rid herself of that ghost, but no. Just one word, one touch, one kiss, a mind-altering orgasm against Mayor

Thompson's terrace wall was enough to bring back the college-aged girl who had made a mistake... Hell, dozens—*hundreds*—of mistakes because of some weak, hormone-crazed moments during her academic career. Times when she'd hated the man in front of her, but she couldn't help herself and had bent to his every desire, and bent him to hers.

She touched her fingertips to her lips, and they still burned with the feel of his mouth on hers. She'd spent half a decade trying to banish him and his devilish hands and wicked kisses from her mind, and she thought she'd been successful. Yet there was no way to quell the feeling that she wanted nothing more than to take the night further. But part of her still held back. Pushing him away had been the right thing to do, even though her body had screamed at her to comply.

She huffed out a frustrated breath. One moment of weakness had made it all come back at her like a backdraft in a fire. She burned for him, needed him, craved his lips, his fingers, the bulge of his cock that she'd felt pressed against her belly, as he held her close, his hands bringing her to a shatter-ing orgasm. She gripped the arms of her leather chair and she clenched her thighs together. He'd been an amazing lover. They'd learned everything, experimented together, and she didn't think she would survive being with him when he had five more years of experience *literally* under his belt.

A knock on her door startled her, and she whipped around in her chair to face it.

"Come in," she called, not sure if her legs were sturdy enough to stand.

Her assistant, Amy, walked into her office, holding a stack of envelopes. "I've got your mail here, and a courier just dropped this off." she said, holding up an envelope.

"Thanks so much," she said, accepting it with a tired smile.

"You doing okay, hon?"

"I'm tired. I didn't sleep well last night."

"Need some more coffee? I was just about to head down to get some for myself."

Rebecca smiled. "That'd be great. Thanks!" When she was alone in her office, Rebecca tackled the large stack of mail on her desk. There were some invites to corporate functions, some junk mail, but it was the envelope that had been couriered, which bore a return-address label for Collins/Fischer, that caught her attention. Using her letter opener, she sliced open the envelope.

Her mouth dropped when she read the letter enclosed, and she knew that it had also gone out to the rest of the shareholders at Daniels International. It was a takeover bid. Brett was initiating a hostile takeover of her father's company.

Shock and rage made her fingers curl over the paper, crumpling the edges. She pushed away from

her desk and stood. She couldn't let Brett get away
with what he wanted to do to her company, the one
her father had worked his ass off to build. She'd told
them that Daniels International was done playing
games with him and Collins/Fischer. She slammed
her fist down on her desk, unable to staunch the
curse words that flowed past her lips.

He'd been irritating her for weeks. Now she was
angry.

Brett and Alex sat in Brett's office on the top floor
of the BH, the office building that was owned by
The Brotherhood. Their mugs of coffee had long
since cooled as the two of them discussed the next
move in the takeover of Daniels International. They
were pleased. Things had moved quickly already,
and he had his amazing partners and their teams to
thank for it. He and Alex had settled on a very generous offer for DI's shareholders. They'd been willing to go far enough above market price so that the
shareholders wouldn't be able to refuse, and they'd
already been contacted by quite a few of them. It
would be only a matter of time before Daniels International fell under the umbrella of The Brotherhood, and they would then move on to dismantling
the next, and then the next, until Collins/Fischer
was the only firm in town. They were on a mis-
sion, and once they were on track, they wouldn't
be deterred. At least, if he kept telling himself that,

he might be able to convince himself that was the only reason he was doing this.

Although Brett had told his secretary he didn't want to be interrupted, she buzzed through on the intercom. "Mr. Collins," she started, "I have Rebecca Daniels on line one. She says it's urgent."

Brett grinned and looked at Alex. She would have gotten her mail and their tender offer already. He couldn't wait to hear what she had to say, and part of him wanted to hear her beg him to spare her company. "Put her through," Brett responded. He kept the phone on speaker as the call was patched through.

"Rebecca, hi—"

"Just what the hell do you think you're doing?" she demanded over the intercom, interrupting him.

"Rebecca, please calm down," Brett said in an attempt at placating her.

"*Please*, go fuck yourself!" she retorted. Brett and Alex both widened their eyes in surprise at the vitriol in her words, but she wasn't done. "So what's your plan here? You make me come and then take over my business?" Brett shot a quick look at Alex, who raised an eyebrow, trying to hide his smile. He didn't try that hard. His friend was clearly enjoying the show.

Brett reached out to pick up the phone receiver, to allow them a little privacy, but Alex swatted his hand away from it. He wanted to keep listening.

"It's just business, Rebecca," Brett said. "It's not personal. It's a strategic move for our own company. This sort of thing isn't unheard of." He stood, unsure of why he was putting space between him and her voice on the intercom.

"This is plenty personal," she said, her voice cold. "But you know what, don't bother explaining any further. You should hear this, though. There is no way in hell you'll get your fingers on any part of my father's company, or me, again. Have a nice day," she said before the phone call disconnected.

"Well," Alex said with a smirk. "She certainly hates your guts. Interesting." He sat back, suddenly serious. "Why don't you tell me what's really behind this takeover? There is some personal shit here, isn't there?"

Brett returned to his desk and sat down. He clenched his fists and hoped that Alex didn't see the tremble in them. He was angry. Angry she still had the power to affect him, like she had years earlier. Sure, the past few months had been interesting—invigorating even—to have his former rival back in town pushing his buttons. But if their encounter the other night had told him anything, it was that she was a distraction big enough to throw him off course—and Brett had come too far and worked too hard to let that happen. He'd created a life for himself around specific things: his work, his business goals with The Brotherhood, staying fit, keeping up with his parents... There was no room for anything else. Certainly not for Rebecca Daniels, one of the few people who made him feel vulnerable and exposed—or at least she had once in college. He couldn't let it happen a second time. "There's nothing to tell," he told his friend.

"And what about that part about making her come?"

"Would you believe me if I called it female hysterics?"

Alex guffawed. "I definitely would not."

Brett sighed and sat back in his chair. "Okay, we had a bit of a moment at the party the other night. But business has nothing to do with that. Sure, the idea of a takeover occurred to me somewhat spontaneously. The plan started forming in my head when she left. But I know what I'm doing here. It's business as usual, regardless of anything that Rebecca and I had."

Alex looked unconvinced. "Jesus Christ, man. We've initiated a multimillion-dollar takeover to get back at a girl you used to hook up with in college? Who just happens to be sitting at the CEO's desk?"

"That's not it."

"Then tell me, what is it? Do you want to start seeing her again? Because if you do, this is one hell of a way to get her attention."

Brett's blood burned in his veins. White-hot. "No. I'm definitely not looking to start seeing her." Although he did extend an invitation for her to visit him at the club. He'd be lying to himself if he didn't admit that he was looking forward to seeing her there.

Brett was a man who didn't deal in feelings. And as anger, ambition and desire all raged within him, he had no idea which would be victorious. He just knew that her appearance threw something inside him completely off-kilter and he needed her gone again. If there was nothing keeping her in Vegas, she would surely leave. Getting rid of Daniels International would send her packing back to New York or anywhere else. He didn't really care.

Using every ounce of strength, he reined in his emotions, holding them back with a firm hand. "The timing looks suspicious, I know. But I've had my eye on this type of thing for a while," Brett lied easily to his friend, something he'd never done before. "This move is what's right for us, and you know it. It's part of our overall vision for The Brotherhood."

Alex stood and faced him, challenging. His friend was a strong, imposing man, and he had a slight height advantage over Brett. "I just want all the information, before you put our business and our names—and The Brotherhood—on the line."

"You have nothing to worry about. I know what I'm doing."

CHAPTER FOUR

REBECCA SLAMMED DOWN the phone. *"That shady motherfucker,"* Rebecca said to her empty office, trying her damnedest to bite back a frustrated scream. She gripped the edges of her desk. If she possessed the physical strength, she would have flipped the heavy oak behemoth over on its side.

Her frustration built and she took deep breaths to stop the shaking in her hands. But it wasn't successful. She thought about her father and the business he'd built and how she couldn't let it fall under the command of Brett Collins. She thought about all of the power and influence Brett had in the city. With what Brett was offering the shareholders for their shares, she wondered how many would stick with DI. It was a near-hopeless situation. But it was up to her to save the company. She was on her own on this one.

"I could see him again," she told herself. "Try to appeal to him." And if she couldn't talk him out of it altogether, she would let him know that she wasn't going to take it lying down. If that didn't work, at least, she could hope to get a little dirt on him and his friends. Rebecca wasn't into blackmail, but she wasn't afraid to play dirty if she needed to.

Hours later, Rebecca found herself on the sidewalk in front of Di Terrestres. The exterior of the club was unassuming enough, just like many other buildings located in Las Vegas's downtown financial district. It was located at the bottom floor of their office high-rise, which housed Collins/Fischer along with many other businesses. The sleek gold letters emblazoned on the sign bearing its name weren't out of place in this neighborhood, but the burly bouncers guarding the door in black suits may have been a giveaway. There was a small line of people looking for admittance, and one by one they were afforded entrance. She'd heard about the club, but a Google search had provided only vague information at best. She'd surmised it was exclusive, intimate even, and she figured that if there was anywhere she would find Brett after hours, it'd be here.

Rebecca frowned, glancing up at the tall building once more. As she approached the lineup, she eyed the doormen, who consulted their lists on the tablets in their hands. Brett had told her to come by, but she was certain she wasn't on whatever list they had in front of them now.

The key was to act like she was.

She straightened her shoulders and strolled to the door, bypassing the small lineup, ignoring the annoyed stares of the people she passed. She smiled at a doorman, but he barely looked at her as she approached. "Name?" His voice boomed. He was huge and had a no-nonsense demeanor.

"I'm here to see Brett," she said, not breaking eye contact. "He invited me."

"Name?"

She sighed, feigning impatience. "Rebecca Daniels. If you could just tell him I'm here—"

"You can go right on in, Ms. Daniels," he told her, looking up at her, now smiling.

She tried to stop the surprise from showing. "Really?"

"Rebecca Daniels." He gestured to the screen. "You're on the list. Go right on inside. You'll find Mr. Collins in there."

She schooled her features, not letting her disbelief that it had worked show. "Thank you," she told him, sauntering past, confident as any woman would be to meet a man at his exclusive club.

From the foyer, Rebecca passed through two huge lush black curtains and found herself in the luxurious environs of Di Terrestres. Her eyes widened, impressed. It was dark but not too dark. The walls were covered with more black curtains, and modern chandeliers and small wall sconces cast dim swaths of golden light over the shadows that crept from the corners. Despite the large size of the room, the design and lighting made it feel small, intimate, sexy even, and she clearly wasn't the only one who thought so. She looked around at the couples and groups of people huddled together at the high-backed booths and tables lining the room. Some of them were talking, laughing, and others were locked in intimate embraces, in various stages of undress. She looked around and noticed how the guests touched each other, spoke softly, as if they were lovers. But the faces were familiar, and she recognized many of them as some of Las Vegas's most influential businesspeople, politicians and celebrities. It left her wondering exactly what kind of place Di Terrestres was.

At the center of the room was a huge raised platform, and she imagined it must have been a dance floor, but no one was dancing; the patrons were so wrapped up in each other, it went unused. Her attention returned to the people around her, engaging in extremely private acts in a very public space, and she felt envious, not having been able to give in to her own desires in a long time.

As a younger woman, she'd exhilarated in exhibitionism, and it was Brett who had brought that out in her. Their semipublic physical encounters were still with her. Back then, they'd done it everywhere—the college library, empty classrooms, store changing rooms—and the heat of the memories made her skin flush as it came over her from time to time. She shook her head in an attempt to disperse the images.

Brett was nowhere to be seen in the crowd, but she did see a long bar along one wall and made her way toward it. If she was going to talk to Brett again, she needed a drink…or several. So she took her place on an empty stool between two men, who simultaneously gave her an obvious once-over before they both turned to her with interest as the bartender quickly made her way over to Rebecca. "What can I get for you?"

"Gin and tonic please," Rebecca told her, trying to ignore the attention of the men who flanked her. "A double."

The gorgeous bartender nodded. "You got it." She quickly made Rebecca's drink and placed it in front of her on a cocktail napkin.

Rebecca withdrew her credit card from her purse to pay for her drink, but the bartender shook her head at her and walked away to serve the next customer. Rebecca's eyebrows drew together as she watched the bartender take payment from another customer, and she wondered why she hadn't been charged.

Her question was answered almost immediately when Rebecca caught a whiff of cologne—the spicy, leathery scent she remembered so vividly

from the night of the mayor's party. *Brett's cologne.*
A dim shadow fell over her, blocking the already-
low light, and soon she felt a wall of warm muscle
come up behind her and press against her back. She
stiffened, and the other men turned their attention
back to the bartender, apparently not willing to in-
terfere in Brett's affairs. Brett rested his palms on
the bar on each side of her, trapping her between it
and his chest. She didn't turn around, and she felt
him lean closer, bringing his lips to her ear. "I knew
I'd see you again soon, Becca."

"And I knew that I'd have to remind you again
that I go by Rebecca now." She sighed and looked
over her shoulder at him. He was as gorgeous as
always. In an attempt to steady her shaking hands,
she cupped her glass and took a deep swallow of
her drink. The gin was definitely top-shelf, and
it hit the bottom of her empty stomach. Maybe
she should have skipped the drink—no, going in
sober wasn't an option—or maybe she should have
stopped to eat dinner before going to the club. And
maybe, she thought as she looked up at Brett, either
way she was making a huge mistake.

She needed to keep a clear head, especially when
the memories of the party had clouded every rational thought she'd had since that night. His proximity only made it worse. Her throat dried and she
took a deep gulp of her gin and tonic and turned
back to look at him once more.

He was wearing gray slacks and a white dress shirt, unbuttoned at his throat with the sleeves rolled up, exposing the tanned skin of his strong, corded forearms. His thick dark blond hair was tousled, and a five-o'clock shadow dotted his firm jawline. It looked like he'd left work and come to the club. But it didn't matter what he wore, he looked just as good as he had wearing his more formal blue suit a couple of nights ago at Mayor Thompson's house.

She steeled herself, attempting to hold back her emotions, her desire, reminding herself of the job at hand. But tell that to the breath she held in her lungs and the stirring in her core. She swiveled on her stool, rotating around to face him. He was standing over her, so closely that her knees brushed high on his thighs. While the shock of the contact racked throughout her, he didn't even appear to flinch. But that was Brett—always so cool and in complete control.

"Can I get you a club soda, Brett?" The bartender had reappeared.

"No, I'm good. Thanks, Tanya," he said without looking away from Rebecca.

"You put my name on the list." Rebecca looked up at him. His face was only a few inches from hers. It wasn't a question. He'd obviously done it.

His smile was cocky, his dimples deep. "I did," he said with a nod. "I knew you'd come here eventually. That you couldn't stay away. Especially after Saturday night, I knew you'd be back for more."

"You're unbelievable. You still thought that I'd come here for sex, even after this morning when you initiated a hostile takeover of my company...?"

"You know, *hostile takeover* has such a negative connotation. I'd like to refer to it as a *friendly buyout*."

"Tomato, *tomahto*," she countered.

Brett laughed. The deep notes rolled over her, and he quickly turned serious as his eyes bored into hers. With each breath, she pulled more and more of his masculine, leathery scent into her lungs, until he surrounded her completely, inside and out, and the rest of the room, the lights, the music, the other patrons fell away, ceasing to exist in the bubble that Brett had created around them. She wasn't sure if she needed him closer or to get away from him entirely as her head clouded pleasantly, but her nerve endings came alive. She tried to lean back, but the hard edge of the bar dug into her back, holding her in place.

She tried to keep her wits about her. But it was proving harder and harder by the minute. "What made you so cocksure that I'd want to see you again?" she replied, her choice of words intentional. "And what makes you think Saturday night has anything to do with me coming here tonight?"

His smirk was arrogant, and the corners of his lips

quirked upward. He leaned closer so his murmured voice could be heard over the din of the club. "So you're here to yell at me again? I did like that phone call."

She shook her head. "No, I'm not here to yell. I just want to talk."

"Oh, really? You aren't mad anymore?"

"Make no mistake, I'm mad as hell. What you did was sneaky and underhanded. But I'm here to see if there's anything I can do to persuade you to stop." Rebecca hated the unconscious sensual lilt of her voice, the way her eyes slanted at him, and she tried to hold it back. Brett just brought it out in her, apparently. She could flirt with him, but she wouldn't trade sex for a deal. She wanted to use her words, her business savvy, to convince him to halt his takeover.

"There might just be one way you could convince me," he murmured, leaning in.

"You've got to be kidding me if you think this is going to be another replay of Saturday night."

He shrugged and stepped back, finally giving her the room she desperately needed to breathe. "Can't blame a guy for trying." He looked around. "It's kind of loud down here. Why don't we go upstairs to my office? We can talk."

"Just talk?" she asked carefully.

"If you want to talk, we can talk. If you want to

do anything else, we can do that, too," he finished. His eyes betrayed the meaning behind his words.

And Rebecca tried her hardest to ignore the raw sensuality that flowed from his lips, the pure sex that he exuded from every part of him. She'd tried to convince herself that she was there only to talk to him, but as she got ready at home that evening before heading to the club, she'd still selected her favorite bra and pantie set, and put it on underneath her sensible clothing, as if her body had some idea or hope as to where the evening would go, despite what her mind told her.

Unable to keep her focus on his steel blue eyes, she pulled hers away and looked around, over his shoulder. Trying to distract herself from the sinful promises in his gaze, she leaned back, putting some distance between them. She knew that if she went anywhere alone with him, she'd be finished and would do anything he wanted. She needed to buy herself a couple of minutes before they were alone. "This is quite the club you guys have here."

"We like it." He still didn't look away from her.

But her gaze wavered past him, to the couples and groups in the booths. Even the air was erotically charged, thick and heavy. "Why don't you show me around first? I'd love to get a tour from the owner." Her rational brain thought that, but she knew in her heart that it wouldn't. Going off with him alone would only lead to them naked. She knew it. But it was already too late for rational thought. She was officially a woman led by hormones and the dangerous man in front of her.

He smiled and extended his arm to her. "It'd be my pleasure."

She took it, sliding her fingers over his bare forearm. The thick but silky hair that covered his tanned skin tickled her fingertips.

"So you've clearly done well for yourself in the past five years," Rebecca commented.

He nodded. "And so have you, I hear."

She had done well since graduating and leaving town. In just a handful of years working at a New York real estate firm, she'd worked her way up from a junior consultant position to an executive position. It had originally been important to her to get away from the family business and the Daniels name to make her own way. And she'd been successful. The reputation she'd made for herself had preceded her in all her East Coast business dealings. But now she was back in Las Vegas. "But let's talk about you. Tell me about this club."

She watched as Brett looked around, surveying his domain. "The Brotherhood opened it earlier this year—"

"Wait. The who?"

"The Brotherhood. Me and my friends. It's just a name we gave ourselves when we started out— people I've met from different phases of life. We've all been pretty successful in our respective fields. So we collaborate, invest in each other. We all work together. The name is just a little tip of the hat to ourselves. That we aren't just friends and partners, but *family*."

She shook her head. "Who would have thought you and a group of successful men would run the city."

"Well, not just men. You remember Alana Carter from college? She's part of the group. She even made up the name. We all play very important roles in operations. Neither of us would be where we are now if not for each other."

Rebecca nodded, thoughtful. She remembered the other woman from some college courses that they'd taken together. They'd become close, and even though Alana had been one of Brett's closest friends, Rebecca had considered her a friend, as well. Her heart softened a bit to think they'd remained friends all these years. Rebecca had spent most of her adult life not needing anyone, and she couldn't help but envy Brett a little in that respect. "And the name? Di Terrestres?" she asked, looking around at the richly appointed room, as she thought back to the Latin classes she'd taken as a young woman.

"It goes back to Roman mythology. The name comes from *di inferi*, a cabal of shadowy deities associated with the underworld. There are the gods above and below—" he moved his hand up and down, and then gestured to room as a whole "—but *di terrestres* are the gods of the earth."

"Gods of the earth? How wonderfully modest of you," she said with a roll of her eyes.

He ignored her snide remark, and without warning, he pulled her arm, whipping her around to face him. She gasped as his palms landed low on her back, just above the curve of her ass. His touch was hot and firm. "Why be modest when you can live like a god?"

"So what goes on here, exactly?" Rebecca hated the breathy nature of her voice, and the way Brett's hands felt on her as they traveled lower, smoothing over her rear. He squeezed and pulled her closer, so that she could feel his hard cock against her stomach, and she gasped, the air rushing into her lungs as her heart pounded. She felt a kick of heat low percolate within her. She tried to breathe past the desire and focus on having a conversation with him. "It doesn't look like a normal club, and I couldn't find any information available to the public about the goings-on here."

"There is no information available to the public. Our membership is exclusive. But, really, this is just a place where people come to mingle after a long day."

She stared at him. "Okay, what about over there?" She pointed at the booths along the back wall where people were still engaged in various intimate scenes—clutched in embrace, touching, kissing, whispering. Brett had referred to the guests as *mingling*. They were indeed doing that.

Brett chuckled. "Jealous?" he asked with a smirk, looking right into her, digging his fingers into her ass. "All right. Those are people who are taking advantage of the secrecy and discretion that we offer. People feel safe here, and they can do anything they like without it being leaked to the gossip rags. We also have some suites upstairs, if people feel so inclined to use them and if they want a little privacy...for any purpose. The rooms, along with membership fees, are expensive. But we have concierges who take care of what people need, and whether the rooms are used for sex or for someone to crash in after drinking too much, we don't care about what goes on in them. As long as whatever happens is between consenting adults, it isn't our concern."

"So this is a sex club?"

"No, it's not a *sex club*. It's a social club, for people who like to indulge in more erotic pursuits." His voice was firm and flat. He was obviously getting impatient with her questions. He pointed to the area she'd assumed was a dance floor. "But we also provide entertainment. There are erotic stage shows that happen over there every night. We bring in professionals, and they do things like bondage

demos, fire play, sultry dancing, erotic gymnasts…
And there are some other benefits to membership."

"Like what?"

He hesitated. "That's privy only to members.
For people who want a little more of a public experience."

"You don't trust me to tell me what that is?"

"Not really. No." He winked at her. She saw the
playful glint in his eyes that she remembered.

It was her turn to laugh, and she pushed her
hips against him, pressing against the hard length
behind his zipper. Then he flinched. The movement was so small she almost missed it, and he
covered it quickly.

"Well, if you insist," he relented, his words more
of a breath. "But you have to promise to never tell
anyone."

"What if I did?"

"Then the punishment will be severe," he warned
her, but the corner of his mouth ticked up playfully.
"There are exhibition rooms set up downstairs, for
a more complete, immersive experience. And for
those who like to watch and be watched."

Rebecca saw the heat and mischief in his eyes,
and she was more than interested in what went on
down there, but as she felt a familiar desirous flush
come over her once again, she shook herself free of
it. She almost asked to go see it. *But no.* She had to
keep her wits about her. She was there to talk busi-

ness, not sex. *Right?* As they stood in the middle of the club, his hands on her ass, she wasn't so sure. "Maybe we should just talk business," she offered, taking another look around the club, knowing that nothing would get done as long as they stood in the middle of a three-ring circus of erotica. "Why don't we go to your office now?"

The BH, which The Brotherhood had built, was a prominent fixture of the Las Vegas skyline that housed Di Terrestres, but it was also the base of operations for all The Brotherhood's enterprises. Brett, Alex, Rafael, Gabe and Alana all kept offices and private suites in the building, for the nights they worked so late that it only made sense to stay instead of going home.

Brett walked Rebecca to the private elevator that was for their own use only, and using a special key card, he called it to the club's foyer on the ground floor. They had to wait only a few moments before the doors in front of them parted. Brett gestured for Rebecca to go before him. The doors closed and her scent filled the elevator, and during their silent ride to the top floor, he inhaled it—light and citrusy. Brett's gaze trailed over her as she stepped into the hallway. His eyes traveled over her body and he imagined watching her apply her perfume to her pulse points—the insides of her wrists, behind her earlobes and, as his eyes dipped to the low-cut V of her blouse, between her breasts.

Rebecca cleared her throat, and his eyes snapped up to meet hers. Her arched eyebrow told him that she'd caught him staring. He shrugged in response, not one bit sorry. Despite what he had in store for her, he'd be lying if he didn't admit he was thrilled that she'd shown up at his club tonight. They might be business rivals, former lovers, current enemies, but it didn't mean he couldn't picture her naked. That was one of his privileges as her ex.

He walked out of the elevator and cupped his fingers around her elbow. She shot a glare at him at the intimate contact and pulled away. He smirked and they continued their silent walk to his office, their footsteps the only noise echoing off the walls of the empty hallway. He escorted her all the way down to the farthest door, and using his thumbprint on a scanner, he unlocked it, then opened it with a *click*.

Brett held the door open for her and followed Rebecca inside his office, closing it behind them. His office was silent, away from the noise of the club and the revelry of the Las Vegas Strip just a few miles away, and that was just the way he liked it. He spent most of his time in the well-appointed office, and he was glad he'd gone for luxury and comfort when he'd designed it.

Leaning against the wall by the door, folding his arms across his chest, he watched Rebecca as she navigated his space. She looked around at the photographs of his friends and parents on the shelves, the awards and accolades he'd received from the business community. He'd never brought a woman all the way up to his office before, outside of business hours, for any purpose other than work. That didn't mean he didn't use Di Terrestres for its intended purpose. If he met someone downstairs at the club and the chemistry was right, he had no problem taking one of the available private rooms or going to a nearby hotel. But his office, and the bedroom suite it contained, was strictly his domain. His territory. And now there was Rebecca, a blast from his past, sexy, stunning Rebecca in front of him, surveying one of his most private areas. He knew he was crossing a line for himself, but he couldn't bring himself to care right now.

"This is your office, huh?"

He nodded slowly. "It is."

"It's big. Bigger than mine."

It was big, probably bigger than he needed, but he liked it; it impressed his partners and collaborators and it intimidated his competitors. This space, along with his cars, his home, his tailor-made suits and five-hundred-dollar haircut, all combined to portray the image he needed to present. He'd worked hard to create the glossy exterior he showed to the world—it was a reminder to him of his past, of how far he'd come since taking control of his life as a teen addict, and of how differently his life could've gone if he hadn't.

Business was partially about the show, the spectacle. But he couldn't read Rebecca's opinion as he watched her walk over to the kitchenette area, between the wet bar he kept stocked for guests and the espresso machine that was necessary to get him through every day. Despite his refusal to indulge in drugs and alcohol in the past twelve years, he had to admit that he still had his vices, and caffeine wasn't the only one. His other vice was standing next to the small fridge across the room. "You know, as CEO, you can change that," he told her.

She turned to face him and crossed her arms, as well. Her stance was defiant, but the smirk on her face was playful. "I'm not like you. I'm not preoccupied with size. I don't need a bigger office to intimidate anyone."

"Oh, really? And what are your intimidation tactics?"

"My superior intellect. And confidence. You should know I don't take crap from anybody."

He knew that. Oh, boy, did he know that.

"What's through there?" she asked, pointing at the closed door in front of her.

He walked over to where she stood, stepping up close to her, so close that her breasts skimmed his chest. He didn't respond to her question for a moment, and feeling her so close almost made him forget the question. He looked down at her, resting his palms on her shoulders, and then he dragged them down her bare arms. Her skin was like the smoothest silk under his touch. *"Through there* is a bedroom."

Her mouth opened, a perfect surprised O. He could tell the depth of the breath she took when her breasts pushed into his chest. "You sleep in your office?"

"It's just a simple bedroom. And sometimes, if I'm working late, it makes more sense to stay here than to drive home in the middle of the night, just to come back early the next morning." His hands reached her wrists, and then he grasped her hips. "Do you want to see it?"

She rolled her eyes and stepped away from him. She put her hands on her hips and glared at him. "Is this your normal MO?" she asked, taking a step back and quirking a brow. "Meeting women at your club and bringing them back up to your fancy office-slash-bedroom?"

Considering the moment over, Brett also took a step back. "I've never brought another woman to my office for something that wasn't work related. And this is a work-related meeting apparently. So what did you want to talk about?"

"How about hostile takeovers, to start?"

"Okay, what about them?"

"Don't play stupid. It's not a good look for you."

"All right." He folded his arms across his chest. "Then start talking."

"I want to know why you're doing it."

He shrugged. They'd moved seamlessly from a conversation tinged with innuendo to one about work. "We talked about this. It's a good business move," he explained simply. "It's not personal, Rebecca. DI has been our competition in this town for years now. Collins/Fischer is setting itself up to be the biggest real estate development firm in Las Vegas. That means you need to go."

"So you already said. I understand why you're doing it professionally, especially if it's retribution for poaching your executive. But let me tell you, he came to me. I don't run my business with retribution in mind. I'm not interested in games. I'm just questioning the timing of all this."

"You're being paranoid." He waved a dismissive hand.

"I don't think so. Sure, we had some back-and-forth. But the takeover bid shows up on my desk on Monday. Meanwhile your fingers were inside me on Saturday, which was the first time we've actually interacted in person in years. So what's that? Are you trying to tell me that it's all a coincidence?"

"Maybe I was looking for a new project and seeing you again inspired me."

"You're an asshole."

"I'm a businessman."

"Brett, we go way back. We haven't always been exactly nice to each other. In fact, we hated each other, and the only thing we had in common was raw attraction and mutual orgasms. But if this is some sort of game you're playing because we used to sleep together, I thought you had more integrity than that."

"Believe it or not, Rebecca, I didn't spend those years pining for you, wishing to get balls deep in your sweet pussy again, okay? Nor did I spend it thinking about you at all." His lips clamped together stubbornly, before he revealed that it was a lie. He had thought about her. Maybe they hadn't been friends, maybe they hadn't even liked each other at all, but there was something about Rebecca Daniels that had always drawn him in. She was the one who came to him when he was alone in the middle of the night and couldn't sleep. Hers was the face he pictured as he pushed his hand under the blankets and fisted himself to get some relief. She was one of the first people he'd ever told about his high school addiction after starting college. One late night in the darkened business library after they'd hooked up again. He'd never been so open before, and that alone made her stand out, threw him in a way he wasn't used to, even back then.

She huffed out a frustrated breath next to him. He was close enough to feel the warm air on his face. "You know I'm never going to let you take over my father's company, *my company*, right?"

"You can try to stop me, but you've seen the price we're offering your shareholders. I know that DI has been underperforming in the past couple of years. Do you think you can beat it? Think you can hold on to your shareholders?"

She visibly straightened. He knew that she couldn't. "I'll find a way."

"And I don't have a definitive number, but I know that our offer has already been accepted by several of your shareholders. Did you know that?" He took a step closer to her. "It's not too late, you know. You could just sign over your shares to me now. The premium we're offering above market price is a fair one."

"You think I'm just going to sign over my ownership of Daniels International? I knew you were arrogant, but to think that I would just turn my back on my family name… This is something else."

"So why are you here?" he asked her, his chest growing tighter. With anger? Frustration? Desire? He had no idea. "Why did you come here tonight?"

"To *ask* you—because of, or in spite of, everything between us—to stop what you're doing. Reconsider."

"If you think I'm going to do that, you don't know much about me at all."

"I guess I never did know you." She laughed.

A small sad sound that almost made him wrap his arms around her. "I know we were never all that close, just two distant enemies who found common ground in sex, but there were moments when I really thought that we had a connection. And on Saturday night, out on the terrace…" She shrugged. "I don't know, I thought there might still be that small something there between us. I guess I was wrong."

Brett looked away from her. For a brief moment, a regret for the sadness he'd put on her beautiful face crept through him. But he tamped it down. She was playing him, using their past against him, and feelings had no place in business. "There was something," he said matter-of-factly. "I made you come," he said. He reached for his belt buckle, not wanting to think too much about the way his dick hardened in his pants. "So what? You want another go? I'd be down for that. I've got some time to kill."

"Fuck you," she bit out. "You know, I thought you could be reasonable. Maybe not destroy a company my father worked his ass off to build, just to—I don't know—to beat me."

She stalked past him, and before he could stop himself, he reached out and grabbed her wrist, stopping her. "Wait!"

"Let go of me," she said as she whipped around and slapped her hand to his cheek. As her open palm met the side of his face, the sound cracked through his office and they both stood still, looking at each other. The anger in her eyes mirrored that in his, and their chests heaved in tandem with heavy heated breaths.

He could still feel the sting of the slap, but he held her wrist and yanked her to him. She came easily, and with not even a hairbreadth between them, her breasts were pressed tightly against him again.

"What do you want?" she asked him. Her tone was wary, but her eyes were alive and danced with fire.

The fight between the conflicting emotions within him died out as desire came out victorious. There was nothing else he could do but give in to it. "Right now?" he breathed after several beats of silence. "I want you."

Rebecca was acutely aware of the rise and fall of her breasts with every heavy breath she took. His declaration had caused her heart to stutter in her chest. "And I guess you still always get what you want?" she managed to croak as her chest compressed.

He didn't hesitate. He looked down at her, and she met his gaze head-on. "Always."

Brett's mouth crashed into Rebecca's, and despite her hesitance at first, she quickly yielded to him, almost melting in his arms, falling against his body, as his arms tightened around her waist.

He kissed her and, taking her bottom lip between

his own, he nibbled lightly. She gasped, and when her lips parted, his tongue took great advantage and plundered inside. He searched her mouth, and he tasted as potent as he ever had. Their teeth mashed, tongues met, twisting and dueling, mouths stealing each other's air until Brett had to pull away. He dragged his lips across her smooth jaw and down her throat, nibbling her skin lightly, biting, licking, before he took her lips again.

Rebecca was gone. Business was the last thing on her mind. His lips broke away from her mouth and attacked her exposed throat again with the same vigor. "Fuck," he whispered in her ear. "You still taste so goddamn good. If your mouth tastes this sweet, I wonder if your pussy still tastes as good."

His voice made her tremble, and he held her tighter. Memories flashed through her mind. Pictures of them together half a decade ago. His lifting her, pressing her against the wrought iron fence bordering the academic quad. A cool nighttime breeze rushing over her, rustling the leaves on the tree they'd hid under, his palm over her mouth to stop her from screaming in pleasure while he'd entered her.

He palmed her breasts and walked them until they bumped the counter of his small kitchenette. Brett's hands smoothed down her sides and reached around to grab her ass. He squeezed her, kneading her through her skirt, rough, demanding. He grasped her waist and lifted her onto the marble countertop between the sink and the espresso machine.

With a hand on each of her knees, he pushed her legs apart and stepped between her spread thighs. His fingers crawled up her bare thighs until they hit lace. She was wet, and she knew it pleased him. He smiled and stroked her. Moaning, Rebecca arched her body into him and, using two hands, he ripped the slight piece of lace from her body. He let the wasted fabric fall to the floor.

"We don't exactly have an audience, like I know you want." His voice was hoarse, heavy with lust. "But maybe next time."

"Next time?" she breathed, throwing back her head, exposing her throat, where he kissed and nipped at the sensitive skin there.

He raised his head, looking at her. His eyes darkened to indigo-colored pools. "Oh, yeah. You'd better believe there's going to be a next time."

Rebecca sat on the counter, her thighs bracketing his hips, completely open, surrendered to him as she watched his eyes take in her still-clothed body. He was exploring her, using the image of her for his own pleasure and giving it in return. His palms found her breasts again and he squeezed. Her nipples—stiff, needy peaks—protruded through the thin lace of her bra and the silk blend of her dress. Through their impatience, some of the buttons of her shirt had come undone, and her open shirt was as much an invitation to him as were her parted thighs. He pushed her shirt aside, ducked his head and, through the lace of her bra, trapped one of her turgid nipples between his lips. Rebecca cried out as his tongue flicked the bud through the material. She knew each of the noises she made urged him on as they always had. He increased the suction and pressure, and she bucked against him. Wanting—*needing*—more.

His hands rested on his belt buckle and he loosened it, then lowered the zipper of his pants. When he reached into his boxer briefs and pulled his dick out, her eyes widened, anticipating what it would feel like to have him fill her again.

"Condom?" she breathed.

He nipped at the base of her jaw, then reached into his back pocket and withdrew his wallet. He took out the condom. "We're covered," he murmured against her skin.

"Convenient."

"I put it there after I saw you at the party. I knew I'd have you again. I knew the occasion would arise."

"The opportunity isn't the only thing that rose," she said, grasping his cock with her fingers. He moaned out a chuckle against her skin, and his breath warmed her as he went about nuzzling, kissing, biting the heated skin of her throat and shoulders as he rolled the condom over his rigid length. The stubble of his five-o'clock shadow scratched against her skin like sandpaper, but she didn't care. He grabbed her hips again and pulled her to him until the stiff column of his cock met her pussy. He held her in place, but she strained against him, hoping to speed up. But he held her still, teasing her, sliding himself over her bare flesh. Nudging along her lips toward the slick, needy flesh of her core. The delicious friction of his cock skating over her clit was wonderful, and it caused her to cry out. It took only a few strokes to bring her to orgasm, and she came, a bright light flashing behind her eyes. Arching her back, she pushed against him. But he kept up the same motions, staying with her until she quieted.

"Oh, God," she whispered, her breath as shaky as her body while she came down from her orgasm. He hadn't even entered her yet, and she was completely at his mercy.

"I'm not done yet," he promised, pushing his cock into her in one smooth, solid thrust.

He filled her completely, and she gave a loud yell. She felt herself grip him, squeezing him, and the sensation attacking her already-wrought senses was almost too much for her. He buried his face in the crook of her neck, and she wrapped her arms around his shoulders, pulling him closer as she inhaled the leathery scent of his cologne. It was heady, masculine, but it paled in comparison with the innate scent of him. He surrounded her, taking her over so that she could barely think. Instead, she let instinct take over. Accepting him, lifting her hips, meeting his every thrust. He moved his hips back and forth, driving into her, a dance they knew as well as any other, and she surrounded him in turn, pulling him in. She felt the tension tightening like a spring inside him. Her breaths quickened and his movements become more frantic, and from the way he ground his teeth, she knew he was close.

For the second time that evening, Rebecca came, throwing her head back against the cupboard door behind her. Brett's hips pumped quickly, until he stilled above her and let go with a loud grunt, burying his face in her hair.

With Brett's weight and warmth pleasant against her, Rebecca sighed as her arms circled his neck, holding him in place. They were both silent for a moment, fighting valiantly to regain their breaths. Rebecca couldn't move. She was paralyzed by both the postcoital haze and lethargy that came over her, but she was also trapped by Brett's grip on her. She found it tough to form a coherent thought, let alone a sentence. So she didn't even try. She closed her eyes and just focused on breathing and the bliss of their encounter, before the real world came back to them.

The calm lasted only a few seconds, and Brett

pulled his face from the spot between her neck and shoulder to look at her. For a moment, she saw something, a familiar glimmer of what they'd sometimes shared after sex—a nearly imperceptible moment of intimacy—but then his eyes hardened and he pulled away from her, taking several steps back, putting physical and emotional distance between them. He exhaled a rough breath as he drove his fingers through his hair, pushing it off his forehead.

Not sure if her knees would support her, she lowered herself from the counter, using the hard surface to support her weight as she straightened her clothes. Brett quietly disposed of the spent condom and zippered his pants.

Her senses restored, she felt deflated, disappointed. She'd meant to come here and appeal to Brett to stop the takeover of her business, but her hormones had gotten the better of her. When he turned back to her, his posture was rigid and hard. His mouth set firmly. She narrowed her eyes in response and squared her shoulders, trying to retain some semblance of dignity and normalcy, and she finally remembered why she was there.

She cleared her throat. "So I'll ask you once again to reconsider your takeover of Daniels International."

He shook his head, not taking his eyes from her. "Not a chance in hell."

"Then I guess we have nothing else to discuss."

"I guess we don't." He busied himself with some papers on his deck, not looking at her. "You can see yourself out."

She gave a short stubborn nod, more of a quick dip of her chin in his direction, and left his office. The floor of Collins/Fischer was empty. Of course it was—it was well past business hours. Thankfully no one was around to catch her "walk of shame." She stopped midstep. She felt worn but energized, disappointed in herself for not sticking to her guns but fulfilled after the best sex she'd had in half a decade. But did she feel shame?

No. "Fuck that," she muttered to herself.

She quickly found the public elevator—not the private one she'd taken to the floor with Brett—and stepped inside. She had to figure out a way to undermine Brett's takeover. There had to be some way that didn't involve her actually being in the same room with him. She clearly couldn't trust herself around him, and she shivered as she remembered the feeling of being pressed against him, taken by him, filled by him. It had been incredible but so not good for business. A shiver danced up her spine, and she looked at her reflection in the mirrored interior of the elevator, seeing the rash on her throat where his rough stubble had scratched against her. Yes, there had to be another way. But she needed a shower first. As long as she could still smell him on her skin, she wouldn't be able to think about it.

After exiting the building, Rebecca looked up and down the street in search of a cab but saw none. She tapped open the Uber app on her phone and was about to find a ride when a black luxury town car pulled up to the curb in front of her and stopped.

The driver stepped out. "Ms. Daniels?"

"Yes," she answered apprehensively.

"My name is Evan. Mr. Collins called me to meet you out here. He wanted me to make sure you got home all right."

"Oh, really?" A laugh stuttered out of her chest. Brett hadn't been too worried about her well-being when he'd coldly dismissed her from his office. "I'll get a cab, thanks." She looked up and down the street and found it dead quiet, almost impossibly so. Not one cab in sight. *Great, the one time that there isn't any traffic around here.*

"Ma'am," he replied politely. "Mr. Collins asked me to drive you home." He came around the car to her side to open the rear door for her.

Before she got in the car, she looked up at the large high-rise behind her, and her gaze went straight to the top floor. Where Brett's office was located. She could see that the lights were still on in many of the windows, and from her vantage point, she couldn't see in any of them. But part of her was aware of Brett's presence, watching her get into the car that he'd called for her, and the driver he'd managed to summon within minutes of her leaving his office. So, feeling saucy and ready to take him on, she smirked up at the building, held up her middle finger in a salute to her former lover/new business rival and stepped into the car.

After watching Rebecca leave with his driver, Brett pushed himself away from the large window of his office. He was tense, but still he laughed, pretty sure that he hadn't imagined her *ladylike* parting gesture. He passed his desk, where the offer letter and information pertaining to the takeover sat. Rebecca was a complication he didn't need. He couldn't fulfill his dreams in this town with her nearby. His attraction to her had always been too heady—he'd never been able to control himself around her. Even as he'd hated her, competed with her for grades, he'd never been able to deny her when it came to sex. He couldn't risk letting an affair muddle his brain with the local competition.

He'd come too far to lose everything he'd worked for. As a teenager, he'd found himself caught in a whirlwind of impulses and behaviors he'd felt too hopeless to control. He remembered the feeling of losing himself, the fear he'd never be the same again as the drugs and alcohol took hold of him, even as he craved more. He never wanted to be there again. It was his parents who had pulled him out of it, and the confidence he'd gained by becoming sober, by saying no to his addiction, had fueled him through college and shaped the man he was today and who he hoped to become. He had to stay on track until he got there.

But being with Rebecca again was… *Fuck!* It was fantastic. She was everything that he remembered and more. Her every movement, her sound, her scent. It had been deeply buried within him, ingrained on his soul, and in one day, one three-minute fuck, a moment of weakness, it all came rushing back. He never ran his business with his emotions—or his dick—and never mixed business with pleasure. He took a deep breath, hoping to break her hold on him. There was no way he could manage the takeover if he didn't keep his libido under control. "That was a one-time thing," he told himself as he headed for the elevator that would take him back down to the main floor of Di Terrestres. "Fuck," he bit out, stabbing the button with his finger as the doors closed. The woman clouded his head, destroyed his focus, ruined his plans. He had to get rid of her, and maybe the take-over would accomplish just that. If he owned her company, why would she stick around?

When the doors pulled apart again, he found himself back in the crown jewel of their empire, and he found his friends without any trouble at their regular table. He took a deep cleansing breath, trying to calm his demeanor before seeing them, and he realized that he could still smell her on his clothes, seeped into his skin. He clenched his fists and joined his friends at their table. He had to wait only a few seconds before the waitress brought him a drink of soda water. He wished like hell he had a drink in his hand as his friends' stares told him they had questions about his absence. Seeing Rebecca again, fucking her in his office had thrown him off guard. His heart still pounded in his chest, and his legs shook ever so slightly. He looked around the table, annoyed by his physical reaction to her but still stuck with an unsated desire for the woman he loved to hate. "Somebody say something," Brett said to the group.

"Where have you been?" Rafael asked him, getting immediately to the interrogation.

"I had to take care of something upstairs."

"Is that something Rebecca Daniels?" Alana asked. "We saw you go upstairs with her."

There was no point in lying. "Yes, I was with Rebecca again." Parched, he took a large swallow of his water.

"And?" Alex asked.

"She wanted to discuss, in private, our takeover bid of Daniels International."

"You didn't think I should be included on any discussions or negotiations?" Alex asked, and Brett could tell that he was still sore about their discussion earlier. He regretted it. At that pivotal moment in the business, Brett needed his partner and right-hand man on his side.

"Don't worry. It wasn't that formal, and it definitely wasn't a negotiation. She just asked me to reconsider. I told her there was no way. The business comes first," he said, attempting to placate them. "It comes before any feelings or nostalgia of what Rebecca and I had."

"You fucked her, didn't you?" Rafael asked him, even though they all knew the answer.

He didn't respond right away, and apparently his silence spoke volumes to the group of people who knew him better than he knew himself.

"And I'm guessing she wasn't successful in getting you to change your mind," Alana said.

"Nope."

"And I take it you guys didn't part on good terms?" Gabe asked.

Brett remembered Rebecca's middle-finger salute. "We did not."

"You don't think that maybe this will just make things harder for us?"

"Since when are we afraid of a challenge?" Brett shot back.

"Okay, man, what if she saw something? Our plans or something sensitive in your office."

"She didn't." Brett was testy and completely disinterested in being questioned by his friends. He sat back in his chair. "You know what? It's been a long day. I'm going to bed."

Alex took the hint, and Brett was grateful that he relented. "Yeah, it has been." He turned back to Brett. "You going home?"

He shook his head. "No, I think I might just stay here again. I've got a 7:00 a.m. working breakfast."

"Again?" Alana asked. "Haven't you stayed here every night the past couple of weeks? Why do you even have a home?"

"It's mostly for appearances." His smile was wry. "It makes my mom worry less." He yawned, though it was mostly for show. He knew he wouldn't be getting much sleep tonight. But he needed some time alone to figure out just what he was going to do with Rebecca Daniels.

CHAPTER FIVE

STEPPING OUT OF the air-conditioned paradise of her car into the high-noon, one-hundred-degree desert air was not something Rebecca had missed about Las Vegas. And for a few moments, she found herself wishing for the East Coast and its milder temperatures. She fanned her face with her hand, finding it ineffective, as she made her way to the main entrance of the building that housed Daniels International.

Her gait was gentle. She was sore and slightly bruised from how Brett had taken her roughly the night before. But despite the discomfort, her stomach still fluttered a little when she remembered it as one of the hottest encounters she'd had since their college-days hookups. Despite that he'd made her body sing out in rapturous exaltation, she hadn't been able to convince him to abandon the takeover; and her company and the livelihoods of everyone she employed still hung in the balance. She couldn't allow another lapse in judgment. She didn't have that luxury.

She couldn't help but wonder why Brett was doing this. He didn't owe her anything, but she really thought her appeal to his conscience last night would've made him stop and think about what he was doing. They'd always seen each other as rivals, but there'd been a time when she thought they might have hit on more.

There was always something about Brett, though. They'd always shared some kind of connection, and it wasn't just about sex. It was in the moments while straightening their clothes, both tired but also wide-awake, exhilarated from a stellar sexual encounter. It was in those moments of closeness they would let their guards down, and she and Brett had shared things—him, his drug addiction, and she, her feelings of inferiority and never measuring up to her father.

After finding out about his past, she'd admired him more, understood his drive, and he hers. They still battled, but it was not driven by animosity, but by respect and competition…and maybe a little animosity.

Rebecca walked into the elevator and pushed the button for her floor. Thankful for the privacy, she let herself slump, exhausted, against the back wall of the elevator. She had barely slept the night before, and then she'd spent the morning meeting with different shareholders, hopefully convincing them to hold on to their stocks and not sell to Collins/Fischer. She'd been insistent, appealing to each one's history with the company and their relationships with her father, but she hadn't gotten one explicit agreement not to sell. She would have to come up with another plan. One that would put her in firm control. She wasn't going to let Brett pull everything out from under her. Not without one hell of a fight.

What was to be done with a man like Brett? He hadn't responded to her appeal to his feelings. They'd fought the night before, and if the past few months had revealed anything, it was that there was still a lot of bad blood between Daniels International and Collins/Fischer. On both sides. He was mad. But goddammit, she was mad, too.

Even if she was angry at him, she was livid at herself—she was weak in falling for him again last night. But it couldn't have been helped. He'd looked so good, smelled so good, tasted even better…even though she should have been engaged in battle, she'd lost her focus. It wouldn't happen again. Brett Collins was going to find out that she would no longer be distracted.

When the elevator opened on her floor, she walked to the DI office and greeted her assistant, Amy.

"Good morning, Ms. Daniels."

Rebecca smiled. She'd told Amy to call her Rebecca, but Amy had told her that she'd always called her father Mr. Daniels. It seemed as if old habits were hard to break. *Yeah, tell me about it*, Rebecca thought wryly as she accepted the stack of messages she'd received that morning.

She thanked Amy and went into her office. She shuffled through them on the way to her desk and frowned when she found that several were from shareholders, old friends and close colleagues of her father's, announcing their intention to relinquish their shares to Collins/Fischer.

Some of them she'd just seen this morning. How could they have decided so quickly after her requests that they reconsider? Biting back a frustrated cry, she sat heavily down in her father's chair. His desk was large, and she felt like a little girl behind it, like when she would visit him at work as a child, and he would spin her around in his chair. She looked around. The office was still very much her father's. But it should feel like hers. She had to make a change. Perhaps if Rebecca looked and felt more like the leader of the company, everyone else would see it, as well. If she could distinguish her leadership from her father's, let the shareholders know this was just the beginning of an exciting new era at DI, they'd be willing to hang on and give her a chance here, to see what she was capable of.

She buzzed the intercom. "Amy?"

"Yes, Ms. Daniels?"

"Can you please get me some contacts for local interior designers? I'm making some changes."

Even though Brett had gotten an early start on his day, the moon was high in the night sky when Rafael suggested he and Alex join him at the gym for a late-evening CrossFit workout. It was difficult to pull himself away, but he relented; there was no better way to release the tension than with a good, high-intensity workout. *Well, there's one better way*, he thought as the image of being deep inside Rebecca flashed through his mind.

But exercise wasn't effective. He still carried the anger and tension from the previous evening and day. His mind wandered, shifting back to Rebecca. He'd been distracted, and it had made for a frustrating day. Even though he failed to expend all the negative strain on his body, he was glad to get out with his friends. After their regular vigorous routine, Brett, Alex and Rafael headed for the sauna to rest their fatigued muscles, and minds, with a little dry heat.

Brett gripped the towel that wrapped around his waist, and he sighed when he finally sat on the treated wood. Immersed in heat, his muscles relaxed all at once. He wasn't sure how he'd gotten through the workout as he was exhausted from a lack of sleep the night before. He'd tossed and turned in bed with the sexual tension that still burned within him. His mind had been ready to shut down, but his body wouldn't rest. He couldn't concentrate on anything besides the image of Rebecca the night before, her legs spread, arms around him and could still feel her under his hands, smell her on his skin. He'd showered that morning, scrubbed twice, but there was no way to rid himself of her, or what they would have done together.

The sauna was empty as he sat with his friends along a far wall. Rafael looked over at Brett. "You were a bit slow during our session," he commented.

"I'm just tired. I didn't get a lot of sleep last night."

"Me neither," Alex added. They hadn't revisited the issue of the takeover and his *meeting* with Rebecca.

"Are we going to do this again?" Brett asked, drained.

"No," Alex said simply. "If you know this is the right move, that's enough for me. I trust your judgment, unless you give me a reason I shouldn't."

"Thanks."

"Isn't it nice when we all get along?" Rafael laughed.

Brett didn't comment.

"Dude. So, what *is* going on between you and Rebecca?" Alex asked.

"Nothing," Brett answered with a shake of his head. He should have known that he wouldn't get away without being questioned by his friends again. "Like I said, she came to the club last night to see if we would back out of the buyout." He looked at Alex and Rafael and could tell they both knew there was more.

"And?"

Brett blew out a breath. "We had sex."

"That was obvious," Alex answered. "How was it?"

"It was great. It was a lot of fun."

"It was fun," Rafael repeated, nodding. "How unexpected," he joked. "I've never had sex for fun before. I might have to give it a try."

Brett and Alex both laughed. "You're such an asshole," Brett told him. "But I have to amend my previous statement a little. It was great until I brushed her off, sent her away and she flipped me off as she got into a car."

Alex laughed before growing serious again. "But do you think she can jeopardize the takeover?"

"She's already told me that she's going to fight it. I know she's tenacious, and she'll do anything to get what she wants." He shrugged. "But really, I don't know much about her approach to business these days. We weren't exactly close back in college, and I haven't seen her in five years. But I do know that she's tough. I did a little looking, and she's got a rep in New York. A lot of guys think she's a bit of a shark. I don't think she'll make it easy." It was almost admirable that she'd been such a figure in the New York City business world. It proved Rebecca was intelligent, driven, ambitious and would be a huge pain in his ass. Brett closed his eyes, suddenly drained. He dragged his fingers through his damp hair and wondered when the last time was that he'd taken a vacation.

Rafael blew out a breath, appearing to relax in the heat. "You know, we should all go away sometime," he said as if reading Brett's mind. "Take a vacation."

Brett looked over at his friend, taking in the deep frown lines that marked his face, and he wondered if Rafael's political life and future run for mayor were beginning to take a toll on him. Brett knew that Raf was just as overworked as he was. They all were. "Yeah, that'd be great," Brett agreed. "Where are you thinking?"

"I don't know. Rio, maybe? Bangkok? Amsterdam? Gabe's grandmother owns that vineyard in Portugal. We can go anywhere."

Brett nodded sagely. A trip anywhere with his best friends would be amazing. "It's been too long since we did something like that. Let's make it happen. When we close this takeover of Daniels International, that is."

"Yeah, and when I'm mayor of Las Vegas," Rafael

agreed, and Brett laughed, knowing that they would probably never get to take a group vacation, with all of their busy lives and schedules. So he leaned back, and they enjoyed the sauna and the quiet camaraderie. Quiet moments were few and far between for them.

"So, what are you going to do about Rebecca?" Rafael asked.

Brett didn't answer right away. *What should I do about Rebecca?*

"If she's a shark like you suggest, she's definitely going to complicate matters for us," Alex said.

And sex was complicating things further… "I've got to stay sharp," Brett said finally. "Sex has always been the main thing between us. I wouldn't be surprised if she decided to use it as a weapon against me. Hell, maybe that was her aim last night… Maybe she's planning to distract me somehow, use our chemistry to get me to back off." Brett caught Alex's raised brows and the look he sent Raf, who shrugged. If that was her goal, he almost couldn't blame her… He might try it himself if the tables were turned. "Maybe I'll play her game."

"What do you mean by that?" Rafael asked.

"I'm going to use sex to distract her during the takeover. Take her off her game and scoop DI out from under her. But I might as well have a little fun, too." He grinned at his friend. "I'm going to see her again. Soon."

CHAPTER SIX

IT WAS LATE Friday evening when Brett unlocked his
door and walked into his home. It had been almost
a week since they'd begun their takeover of Daniels International, almost a week since Rebecca had
come back into his life—in the flesh. It had been a
long seven days, and work on their DI bid and their
many other contracts had kept him in the office,
in meetings, buried in literal stacks of paperwork,
which had caused him to spend every night in his
office. He'd gotten away only long enough to take
in a few quick workouts and working lunches.

Rebecca was a formidable opponent, and she'd
proved to work just as hard to hold on to her company as he was working to take it from her. She had
somehow managed to keep many shareholders on
board, which was a true feat, considering the price
Collins/Fischer had offered. Brett figured that he
and Alex would have to up the price soon.

He threw his shoulder bag and jacket on a stool
in the kitchen and walked into the living room,

the motion-sensor lights turning on as he went. Everything in his home was just as he'd left it when he'd last been here. The place was neat, tidy, sleek, modern—he barely spent enough time in his home to clutter it up.

He flopped down on his couch. Even though he was exhausted, a particular energy coursed through his veins. He'd told his friends he would find out what Rebecca's game was once and for all, and turn it against her. But he hadn't been able to find any time to do that. Not that he thought she'd even see him, considering how busy she must be, trying to save her own company, and the way they'd parted earlier that week.

Despite not having seen her for days, his thoughts seemed to turn to her without hesitation. He could still feel her, smell her, and a fresh wave of desire came over him. He tried to fight it off, remembering that Rebecca was probably trying to play him, distract him from his plans, but that didn't stop his dick from getting hard in his pants.

God, he'd fucked her, but that ache pulsed throughout him, and he couldn't quell it. He dropped his hand to his lap and palmed his stiff length through the material of his pants. He sighed and leaned back on the couch, figuring that he might as well just jerk off and go to bed. But as he ran his hand over himself, it had no effect on his need, so he pulled out his cell phone from his pocket. He would need a little assistance.

He opened his contacts and scanned through the list of women whose numbers he'd collected. Women with whom he'd previously enjoyed some wild nights. *Kristy, Alexa, Samantha, Bianca...* He let out a frustrated sigh when he realized that none of them would do. There was only one woman who consumed his mind, and she certainly hadn't given him her cell number.

Wanting to get to the bottom of all the questions he had about her to find a way to weaken her position, he opened the internet browser on his phone, and in the search bar he typed "Rebecca Daniels." Her picture, a professional headshot, filled the screen, and he lingered over it. She looked confident, composed. Shiny blond hair and radiant blue eyes. But he couldn't help but see her sensual side. The side of her that got off on being fingered at a party. Her social media accounts were also listed, and he found her Facebook page. Should he message her? He clicked on the private messaging app, but he paused in hesitation before he typed, then dashed off a quick message and sent it before he could hesitate.

I want to see you.

It was true. While he tried to tell himself that it was strictly business, it wasn't. Part of him wanted to see her, to throw her off her game. Getting her out of the way would definitely make his life easier. But as his dick ached, and his libido took over, he knew those weren't the only reasons he wanted to see her.

He could tell that she'd seen the message, and the three telltale dots showed that she was writing a message.

Why?

Call me a masochist.

You aren't the only one. Why are you still awake?

I just got home. I can't sleep.

Me neither. I haven't been home long myself.

He paused, knowing she was working just as hard as he was to stay cool, before he continued typing. Why don't we get a late dinner? We can talk.

It's late.

I know.

Christ, it sounded like he was begging. Brett never begged.

Just to talk?

I swear. He looked at his phone. There was no movement on the screen. Then the three dots danced in the message window. He held his breath, stilled, feeling like a statue as he waited for her reply.

Where do you want to go?

Just give me a minute to make a phone call. I know a place.

Rebecca parked her car outside Thalia, the restaurant Brett had selected. The parking lot was empty, and she wondered if the place was even open. It *was* eleven at night—definitely late for dinner.

A black Porsche, shiny under the lights of the parking lot, pulled in after her. It parked and Brett got out. He was still wearing a suit, but it was slightly rumpled and she knew it must have been the one he'd been wearing all day.

The corners of his lips turned upward a little. A small, imperceptible movement, but she remained cautious. "I don't think it's open," she called to him as he neared.

He looked up at the building and frowned, making a show of checking his watch. "No. I don't suppose it is." But he continued walking to the door.

He pulled it open and waited for her to walk ahead of him.

The restaurant was completely empty, and a server appeared before them. "Mr. Collins, Ms. Daniels, thank you for joining us this evening," the man said with a smile.

Rebecca wasn't sure how happy he must be with the latecomers. She hoped they weren't putting any of the staff out by showing up at this hour.

"Thanks for having a table for us," she replied with a gracious smile. Looking up at Brett as the waiter showed them to their table, she wondered what kind of pull he had with the owner to accommodate them so late. But she shouldn't have been surprised. Brett's influence in the city was strong. They were led to a plush round booth in a far corner. The high back almost completely secluded them from the rest of the empty restaurant.

She slid in, Brett sat across from her and the waiter placed two menus in front of them before taking their drink order—Malbec for her, soda water with basil and lime for Brett, an order the waiter already seemed to know.

They didn't speak until the server returned and put their drinks in front of them. Rebecca studied Brett instead of her menu. She still didn't understand what she was doing there. Why had he messaged her? And why had she been so willing to meet him? They hadn't exactly parted on good terms the last time she'd seen him. She blamed it on fatigue. It had been a long week for her, fighting to keep her company away from the strong hands of the man across the table from her.

He turned back to her and smiled. The gesture didn't quite reach his eyes, and they sat in silence for a moment, just looking at each other as light music played throughout the empty restaurant.

Before long, his scrutiny proved to be too much and she looked away first, taking in their surroundings before drinking a sip of wine. "I'm kind of surprised that you were able to get a table, you know, in a closed restaurant and all," she said over the rim of her wineglass.

"You probably shouldn't be." He smirked.

"This is a nice place. I've heard great things about it."

He looked past her, seemingly surveying the rest of the dining room before sipping his water. "Thanks."

"Of course. You own this place, too?"

"Brett." Rebecca heard a woman call from behind them. She craned her neck over the high back of the booth to see who had called out to him, and she saw Alana approach the table.

He smiled. "Hey, I didn't know you were still here."

"Yeah, I'm heading out now. I just wanted to

make sure that Nick and Josh were okay with staying late for you."

"We appreciate it. Thank you for arranging it."

"Anytime. You just make sure you tip them well for staying however long after close you'll be keeping them."

"Of course," Brett agreed.

Rebecca was relieved that they both would make sure their staff was taken care of. She'd spent summers working in service jobs. Her father had insisted that she get a taste of the "real work that keeps the country going."

Alana turned to face her. "Rebecca, it's great seeing you around again. It's too bad we didn't get a chance to speak yet. How are you?"

"I'm fantastic," she replied. Alana hadn't seemed to change at all from when they were younger. She was always so kind, and Rebecca had really liked her. "And you?"

"So good," she said. "Everything is great but extremely busy."

"I was just telling Brett how amazing this place is. It's a beautiful restaurant. I can't imagine what it must be like when it's actually open," she said, sliding her eyes across the table at Brett.

Alana laughed. "You're kind. Thank you. This place really is my pride and joy. It was the first one we opened." She looked around the room with affection and put her hand on top of the booth above

Brett's head. "She's my baby. It was nice seeing you, but I should go and leave you guys alone." Turning to Brett, she said, "Want to do brunch tomorrow?"

"I can't," he told her. "I'm having my biweekly brunch with my parents tomorrow."

She nodded. "Okay. Tell them I said hi." She turned to Rebecca. "Would you like to get together tomorrow, Rebecca? We can catch up."

Rebecca caught Brett's frown at Alana's invitation but ignored him. Just because she and Brett were at odds didn't mean that she was going to let him stop her from forging relationships with her old friends. "Yeah, that sounds great," she said, pulling her card out of her purse. "My cell number is on there. Just text me when you get a chance, and we can arrange a time and place."

"Awesome," she said, turning back to the direction of the kitchen. "Okay, I really have to go now. Have a great dinner, guys. The porterhouse is a dream tonight, and Josh is a master with beef," she said with a wink before disappearing across the restaurant.

Left alone in silence again, Rebecca turned back to Brett. "Okay, Brett, what are we doing here?"

"I'm thinking about getting the porterhouse," he said, pushing his menu aside.

She rolled her eyes at him. "Why did you ask me to come here?"

He shrugged. "I don't know. I don't feel good about the way we left things the other night. I've been thinking about it all week."

She nodded. "It feels like we have some things to discuss." Although she had no idea of where to start.

The waiter returned and, as per Alana's suggestion, they both ordered the porterhouse.

When they were alone again, she played with the stem of her wineglass for several moments, trying to form the words, before she looked up at him. "So what should we talk about?"

"I'm sorry I fucked you the other night in my office."

She sat up straight. It wasn't exactly the conversation starter she was anticipating. "Excuse me?"

"You heard me. It was great, but it shouldn't have happened. Because since then, I've done nothing but think about how amazing it is to be buried deeply inside you, hear the way you sound when you come. It's driving me to distraction."

She felt heat rise over her chest to her cheeks. She took a mouthful of wine to quench her parched throat. She hadn't expected him to be so up-front about it. "Brett…" she breathed.

"Did you know that you still make the same sounds when you come?"

She blinked rapidly and looked around. The waiter was across the room, but in the quiet stillness of the restaurant, there was no way he hadn't heard what Brett had just said. Stunned for words, she tried her damnedest to form a coherent sentence, to tell him to go to hell, to leave her alone, anything. But she'd already lost. The heat in his darkened eyes burned her as much as his words. She gulped her wine, and with her throat constricting, she almost choked on it. "I, um…" Her words stuttered out.

The waiter, Nick, reappeared. "Would you like another glass of wine?" he asked, eyeing her now-empty glass.

She hadn't realized that she'd completely downed the glass. "Yes, please." When Nick left the table, she took the opportunity to watch Brett. She looked up and saw that he hadn't looked away from her. She needed a break from him, just for a minute. "You know, this looks great, but I have to excuse myself for a moment. I need to wash my hands." She pushed away from the table and stood and thankfully stopped her legs from wobbling as she walked away, shoulders square, head held high.

Inside the bathroom, she blew out a heavy breath and stared at her reflection in the mirror. "You know what he's doing, don't you?" she asked her reflection. "He's trying to get even with you, seduce you. To distract you from saving your company." She had to fight him, but she wasn't sure how when just his words sent her insides into a complete tizzy.

She narrowed her eyes at herself. "But it's never going to happen," she told herself. "You didn't come this far to let some guy take it all away from you. Two can play at that game."

Brett watched Rebecca walk away, the sway of her ass underneath her skirt forcing him to stifle a groan. What he'd intended to be a seduction of distraction had quickly turned against him. He was just as affected, just as turned on as he was trying to make her, and as he willed away the growing erection behind his zipper, he pulled out his phone and saw a missed call from Alex. He returned the call, and after several rings, his friend picked up.

"Hey, what's up?" Brett asked him.

"I know it's Friday night, but something came up."

"What is it?" Brett's voice lowered. "Is something wrong?"

"It's not the end of the world yet, but I wanted to let you know that there's someone else making a run for shares in DI."

"What do you mean?"

"We didn't notice it until today. I don't know who these guys are, but they've got a lot more shares now than they did when we checked last week."

"Who is it?"

He could hear Alex shifting papers over the line. "A holding company called RMD. They're currently in possession of sixteen percent, not a lot, but it's up from ten two weeks ago. And they've put out a standing order for any available shares."

"That's interesting," Brett said. "Who's RMD?"

"I don't know. I couldn't find any information on them at all. I've got our guys on it, but they won't know anything until tomorrow at the earliest, if they find anything at all."

Well, fuck. They hadn't counted on that. "So, with this new buyer on the scene, the pressure is definitely on Rebecca right now."

"Not only her, but us, too."

"Yeah, do you think she can hold on to power?"

"We just have to outlast her and whoever RMD is."

"Well, after tonight, maybe she won't have the focus to hold on to power," Brett said slowly.

"What, you're going to fuck her senseless again?"

"I'll do whatever I have to do. But I will gladly take this bullet for the team." He raised his eyes and saw that Rebecca had silently made her way back to the table. "I've got to go. Let's talk tomorrow." He put his phone away and smiled at her. "All good?" he asked, wondering how much she'd heard.

"Yeah," she said. Her face was emotionless and impassive. She slid gracefully into the booth and, surprising him, she moved in farther and sat next to him instead of in the place she'd once occupied across from him. She reached across the table for her wineglass, leaning into him more than she needed. He inhaled, her scent driving him mad, filling his lungs as his body stirred in response.

Rebecca pivoted her upper body so that she faced him. "You look tired, Brett," she purred, before taking a sip and eyeing him over the rim of her glass. "You getting enough sleep?"

"Don't worry about me," he told her. In fact, he hadn't been getting enough sleep. But as he watched her take another sip of wine, he didn't care if he ever slept again. How he wished that he was the glass that was pressed between her lips. Swallowing back the groan that threatened to pass through his lips, he cleared his throat and took a large mouthful of water.

"You okay?" she asked, bringing her hand to his chest to toy with the top button of his shirt.

"Yeah," he managed. "Couldn't be better."

"Listen, Brett," she said, her voice husky. "We might have different priorities when it comes to business, but we were always good together, weren't we? Like when we would meet up in our special spot in the business library?" She loosened his top button, pushed the material open and swirled her fingers in the hair between his pecs.

Her touch was welcome, but it caused his heartbeat to ramp up. He chuckled. "I know what you're doing," he warned her, grasping her lithe fingers in his.

"And what's that?" she asked under her breath, her eyes wide and innocent.

"You're using sex to get me to call off the take-over."

"I thought you said it was a buyout," she murmured before pulling back. "And do you really think I'd do something like that?"

In response, he dropped his hand to her thigh and squeezed. She parted her legs ever so slightly, allowing him better access to the smooth, butter-soft skin of her inner thigh.

When his fingers traveled inward, the tips circling against her skin, her lips parted, and for a moment she looked lost and distracted. But she moved past it and her eyes found his, and they were sharp. "To be honest, Brett, I don't think I'm the only one who's playing that game, am I?"

His fingertips found the silk of her panties, and her eyelids fluttered close. "You aren't." He slipped his fingers underneath and found her wet.

Rebecca pushed her head against the back of the booth. "So maybe we should just cut the crap for tonight and admit why we're both here."

"Sounds good to me," he said, his voice rough, and he grasped her waist and pulled her onto his lap so her thighs straddled his hips. There was barely enough room between his front and the table, but

Rebecca fitted there, pressed against him. His hands smoothed up her back and he cupped her cheek and the nape of her neck. He looked at her, and they shared a powerful moment, but he pulled her to him, drawing her mouth to his.

His tongue snaked against her lips, and she opened to him. Their tongues swirled together. He searched her mouth, taking in her completely intoxicating flavor. When her arms encircled his neck, he released his hold on her face and palmed her breasts, squeezing as she arched against him and moaned into his mouth. He went lower, and his fingers were under her blouse, cupping her over her bra.

Breaking glass startled them, and they pulled apart. Brett's hand was still up her shirt when they turned their heads to the bar of the restaurant to see Nick standing there, looking at them. Brett had forgotten all about the waiter and the chef who were still in the building, and almost nothing would have stopped him from fucking Rebecca in the booth.

Nick was flushed, probably from the show that Brett and Rebecca had put on. Brett knew the man was a professional and could be counted on to be discreet, but that didn't mean he should be a witness to the show. Nick looked at them. "Can I offer either of you another drink? The food will be out momentarily," he said, not coming closer to the table, still trying to do his job but also giving them privacy.

Brett turned back to Rebecca, who was still on his lap, wedged between his chest and the table. "Are you hungry?" he asked, barely able to squeeze the words from his chest.

She swiveled her hips against him, the friction sending a powerful bolt of need through his body, all the way to his limbs. "I'm starving."

He grinned, knowing she wasn't talking about food. "Why don't we just get out of here?" She nodded, and he helped her off his lap and said to the waiter, "Nick, thank you for everything, but we're going to head out. Can we take it to go?"

"Very good, sir."

Nick left the dining room and came back a few minutes later with the food wrapped—Brett knew they didn't normally offer takeout, so he appreciated it all the more.

Brett stood, fished out his wallet and pulled out several hundred-dollar bills, and passed them over to Nick. "We appreciate you guys sticking around for us, but we've kept you long enough." He grabbed the food with one hand, wrapped his arm low around Rebecca's waist and ushered her to the door. "Let's go."

When Brett escorted her out of the restaurant with a firm hand on her lower back, she could feel his power, and the tension, just from the placement of his fingertips. And even though she was determined to play and win his game, the minute he touched her, she had to fight for every intelligible thought. She looked at her BMW parked on one end of the parking lot, and then at the black Porsche 911 he'd arrived in. He was steering her in the direction of his.

"My car is here," she told him.

"You can get it in the morning."

In the morning? There was no doubt that they would be spending most of the night together, but she never imagined he would want her to stay. She nodded as he unlocked the car with a beep, and he opened the passenger-side door.

"Cool car," she said as he settled into the seat next to her.

"Thanks," he said. "I know it's a bit flashy, but I like it. It's fast."

"If you can't be flashy in Vegas, then where?" she said, flattening her hands over the sleek leather of the console. "I think it's sexy."

"And this is a city built on sex," he said, starting the ignition. He smoothly pulled out of the parking lot and started down the road.

Struck by a memory, she giggled. When he turned a questioning look in her direction, she continued to laugh. "Remember the semester we got stuck as partners working together for that big operations assignment?" They'd spent so many hours and late nights working on the semester-long project, that soon the pressure and proximity, not to mention the constant head butting and arguing, had gotten to them. It marked the beginning of their fling.

"Yeah. That course almost kicked my ass."

"It was tough. It's a good thing I was there to keep you focused."

He chuckled. "Focused? If I recall correctly, the only thing we were focused on was getting naked."

"How times have changed," she muttered ironically, reaching for him. She put her hand on his thigh and smiled at the way his jaw flexed in the dim light of the dashboard. "Do you remember the night we stayed late in the business library and you offered to give me a ride home and you almost crashed your dad's Murciélago?" Her fingers danced upward, and she found him hard. She gripped him, and he tensed, laughing roughly.

"I remember taking his new Lamborghini without asking him, and I remember driving too fast. But my dick in your mouth was the thing that almost made me crash it." He chuckled.

It was a stupid thing they'd done. And she remembered how she'd jostled about the front of the car when he had to swerve off the road to avoid hitting a car that had stopped in front of them. Neither of them, nor the car, had been hurt, but it had been reckless and he'd driven her home in silence. But she still wanted to be reckless. There was something about Brett that made her want to be reckless. She looked down in his lap and wondered if the memory of road head had caused the distinct bulge in his lap. Bringing it up had had the desired effect. "We could have been killed," she whispered. "You were driving so fast."

"But that would have been quite a way to go, don't you agree?"

"Do you think your driving's improved any since that night?"

He slid his eyes over to her, and his grip tightened on the steering wheel. "I believe it has."

She didn't respond, but she reached across and dropped her hand into his lap and palmed his semi-hard dick, turning it into a rigid staff. "Want to give it another try?"

He almost veered off the road again, and she smirked when he fought to regain control of the car. He coughed to clear his throat. Hell, if he'd been turned on at the start of this conversation, with just the memory of that night, he was raring to go now. Her hand on his thigh was enough to make him almost burst through his pants.

She licked her lips, a cool move that made him exhale roughly, and she leaned over the console. "Want me to do something about that?" Her voice was low, sultry, smoky. And the sound traveled straight to his dick. He couldn't remember another woman who had been able to make his engine go from zero to ninety in one second flat.

Do I want her to? Was he fucking crazy? Of course he did. He grunted in response and swallowed roughly.

She gripped him, stroking him through the material of his gray pants. He shuddered, which caused her to smile, and he had to focus all of his attention on staying on the road. He pressed down on the accelerator, desperate not to lose control and crash the car.

Rebecca unbuckled her seat belt and leaned over the console. Putting her lips to his neck, she kissed him lightly on the pulse point under his jaw where the collar of his shirt had been opened. She traced his throat in light kisses, in a trail to the open neck of his shirt. Her hands made quick work of his belt, unsnapped his pants and slowly lowered his zipper.

"Rebecca…" He gave her a half-hearted warning. "Maybe we shouldn't… I'm driving."

"So drive," she challenged him, looking up at him. "Don't mind me."

He moaned when she reached into his boxers and pulled out his hard cock. He glanced down and he could already see the glistening drop of precum that hung to the tip. He focused on the road in front of him—and staying on it.

She pulled her hands away and shifted in her seat

so that she was kneeling in the small low bucket seat of his sports car. Her ass was in the air, almost pushed against the window, and he couldn't help himself from removing one white-knuckle hand from the wheel to smooth it down the curve of her spine to her round rear. He gripped it hard and she squealed. He laughed and leaned his head against the back of his seat. Leaning fully over the center console between them, she took him in her hands again. Circling him in her little fist, she pumped several times, each one making him moan in need. But he didn't want her hands. He put a guiding hand on the back of her head and lightly pushed her down, telling her exactly what he wanted, but not using enough force that she couldn't resist if she didn't want to indulge him. "Your mouth," he whispered.

Rebecca moaned in agreement as her lips parted over the head of his dick, her tongue swirling around the crown. He glanced down, but just watching the illicit act was almost enough to make him lose it, so he threw his head back against the headrest and watched the road, noting that they were almost to her family house—he knew she'd be living there now that she was back and her father had passed. He came upon a red light and stopped the car. The tinting on his windows kept the people in neighboring cars from being able to see the lewd activity that was happening only a couple of feet away, but even if they could see, he wouldn't care. Hell, he would have rented out the arena at MGM Grand and sold tickets to the show for how goddamn good it felt.

Her head lowered, taking him deeper into her mouth until he felt himself hitting the back of her throat. And then she still went deeper. *Neat trick*, he thought, amazed by the view of her head in his lap, her lips resting at the root of his cock, and he wondered where she'd learned it. The traffic signal turned green and he peeled off. The lights of the city passed in front of him in long streaks of color. It felt like he was intoxicated, driving drunk. For someone who lived his life in such tight control, he felt like a wild man, and Rebecca brought that out in him.

His hand rested on the nape of her neck, his fingers curling into her hair, feeling the muscles in her mouth and throat cradling him, pressing against him, sucking, drawing every ounce of pleasure from him. He moaned again. His hand smoothed over her shoulders, then back down the material of her sensible knee-length dress, coming to rest on her ass. As long as he didn't need to shift gears, he could keep one hand on the wheel and the other on her. He squeezed his fist in her hair as she pulled back up over him, withdrawing him from her mouth with a quiet pop. With her tongue, she licked him in several long strokes before taking him fully into her mouth again. Rebecca went to work in earnest, her head bobbing up and down. Overcome with the feeling of desire, he quickened his breathing, and from the way his balls tightened, he knew he was close.

"Becca," he breathed. "I'm going to come. Oh, shit. Rebecca, you have to stop."

"Mmm." She hummed in response, her mouth currently too full to speak.

Thankfully, he recognized her old house, and he pulled into the driveway, just as his orgasm overtook him. With one final squeeze of her lips and a stroke of her tongue, he came with a shout and slammed the brakes. He flexed his hips upward, coming in her mouth with heavy spurts of hard liquid. The motion of the muscles in her throat told him she'd swallowed every drop of him as he spasmed with release, and he groaned in relief as he wiped the thin layer of sweat from his forehead.

His grip on the back of her neck loosened, and she sat up, coyly swiping her finger along the edge of her mouth before closing her lips over a cherry-red fingernail.

He'd just come but he needed her again, and he turned off the engine and moved to get out of the car.

"Wait, where are you going?" she asked him.

"Inside with you. We're not done here yet."

"No, Brett, we are."

He blinked. "But what about you?"

"Don't worry about me," she said coolly. "I've got a vibrator if I need it."

"Rebecca…" he implored her, trying to get the image of her using the toy on herself out of his head. "Let me come in. I'll show you a good time."

She shook her head, dismissing him. "Don't worry about it. I never want to feel like I owe you anything. But I want you to know something. That will be the last thing you *get* from me." With a slick smile, she got out of the car and walked into her house without looking back.

Once inside, Rebecca could finally take a breath. She walked up the stairs to her bedroom and wasted no time stripping out of her dress, bra, stockings and drenched panties, and she put on a short silk robe. A needy, unsatisfied mess, she went back downstairs and grabbed a bottle of red wine from the bar, opened it and poured, half filling the glass. She pulled back and shrugged before pouring more, filling the glass to the rim.

With shaking hands, she brought the glass to her lips and gulped. But it was no use. She could still taste him over the profile of the expensive wine. The upper hand she believed that she had with Brett was short-lived, as she felt a white-hot need for him course through her body. Based on what she'd overheard from Brett's side of the conversation he'd had on his phone, and everything she knew about Brett's desire to win, she knew that he had invited her out to seduce her, distract her, and her attempts to turn the tables had left him breathless. But she knew she would have to take care of her own need, and soon; and she'd have to every other time she thought of him.

She headed back up the stairs to bed but got only halfway there before the doorbell rang. Stopping, she turned and went to the door. She looked through the peephole and saw Brett standing on the other side. He stood in profile, looking off to the distance, his hands on his hips. He looked frustrated, annoyed, and when he looked back to the door, it was as if he could look right into her eyes through the peephole, and she was surprised that the heat didn't melt the glass.

She pulled open the door and he was inside in an instant, his arms around her, his fingers grasping, holding her tighter, his mouth hot and crushing against hers. His kiss might have been violent if it hadn't been so full of passion. His lips were hard and demanding against hers, parting hers, his tongue delving deeply into her mouth, finding her tongue, sliding and stroking against hers. She let a moan escape from her throat and into his mouth, and he swallowed the sound and held her tighter, lifting her so that her feet didn't touch the floor.

He tore his mouth away from hers and attacked

her throat with similar vigor, dragging his teeth along the sensitive skin of her exposed throat. He only then seemed to realize that she was wearing nothing but the small robe, and he pulled the material aside, exposing her shoulder and, in the process, loosening the knot of the belt, opening the robe and revealing her breasts.

"Brett," she breathed, unable to say much else.

"Don't say anything," he said. "I just want one more night with you."

"Okay." *One more night.* She could do that. It was what she wanted, too. One night together, and then they could go back to their regular lives as competitors, rivals, enemies. Just one more night of passion. It had been a long time promised, and nothing was going to stop her. Not family or business loyalty, not her common sense. She wanted one more night with Brett. Then she could put it behind her, and she could save her family's company from his greedy hands.

But, oh, those hands...

Brett's eyes flamed and, still holding her aloft, he ducked his head and captured the rosy bud of her nipple between his lips, sucking, nibbling, sending bolts of pleasure shooting straight to her wanting sex. He stayed with her. His tongue swirled over her nipple and she clutched his head, her fingers fisting into his hair. She cried out and wrapped her legs around his waist, shamelessly pushing her pussy against him, and she moaned again, frustrated that rubbing against him did nothing to alleviate the sharp need within her.

With a groan, Brett pulled his head away from her breast and looked up at her. "Bedroom?"

"Upstairs," she breathed. "At the end of the hall."

Still carrying her, he walked up the staircase to the second floor, all the while placing kisses on her neck and shoulders, licking, nipping her skin with his teeth, tasting her.

When he crossed the threshold into her room, she reached out and turned on the light. The dimmer cast a golden glow across the room, and he saw her bed, huge, high, pristine with a white duvet. "Do you realize that this is the first time I'll fuck you on a bed?"

"Does it not work for you?"

"Hell, no. This works very well."

Brett let Rebecca slide down to the floor, and when she stood, he leaned over her and took her mouth with his again. He ripped the robe from Rebecca's body, let it fall. While their tongues and lips danced together, she busied her fingers, tackling his shirt buttons. Impatient, he pushed her hands away and opened it himself. She sat back on the middle of the bed and watched him as he pulled his open shirt from the waist of his pants. In the center of her bed, her hands fisted in the white covering as she watched him undo his belt and whip it from the loops of his pants. He caught the rise and fall of her chest as she refused to take her eyes from his form. Feeling cocky, he paused at the top button of his pants. "Like what you see?" he asked with a smile.

In response, Rebecca placed her palms on her thighs and slid them upward, spreading her legs and revealing herself to him. His smile dropped when one hand toyed with her small triangle of light hair and her fingers dipped between her glistening folds. "You like what *you* see?"

A growl rose from his chest and he fumbled with his zipper without looking away from her. As she played with herself, he quickly shucked his pants and kicked out of them before joining her in the center of the bed.

Brett knelt between her thighs, leaning over her, and grasped her wrist. His hand circling hers, he brought her fingers to his lips. He drew them inside, sucking them into his mouth. Her flavor was sweet and potent on his tongue, and he wanted more. But before he went further, he took another look at her. Rebecca was beautiful, disheveled. A flush covered her chest, and she watched him through heavy eyelids. His dick nudged against her inner thigh, so close to that delicious pussy. It would be so easy to pull her close and take her right then and there.

He wanted it. *Needed it.* But first, he needed to taste her. He eyed her as he went lower, dragging his tongue down her trim stomach, until he reached the apex of her thighs, bringing his face only a breath away from her glistening pussy.

Using two fingers, he parted her sweet lips, diving into her heat. She was molten, wet and ready. Her breath was shallow and she stilled, waiting for his next move. The small, swollen bud of her clit called out to him, and he obliged, moving over her, flattening his tongue against it as it throbbed.

She cried out softly as he touched it, staying still for a moment before flicking it again with the tip of his tongue. Rebecca bucked her hips against his mouth. And he parted his lips and closed them over her. His eyes closed in delicious satisfaction. He tasted her, and she was sweeter than he remembered. He heard her moans as he washed his tongue over her again and again.

Rebecca's hands found his head, and she pulled at his hair. It was painful, but he barely felt it. He was so intent on bringing her pleasure and taking his own by feasting from her that he barely noticed how she pulled on him. He used his fingers to spread her moisture around her, and from the way she yelled out and thrust her hips at him, he knew that she was close to coming. He grinned to himself and put one finger inside her; she tightened around him, and then he inserted another. It was all she needed. She arched and bucked against him, calling out as her orgasm racked through her body.

He held her until her movements quieted and she regained her breath.

With a smug smile, he climbed back over her. His mouth still wet with her, he kissed her, knowing that she could taste herself on his lips. His tongue invaded her mouth, driving against hers. "You ready for more?"

"There's more?"

"You better believe it." He looked over at the bedside table. "Condoms in there?" She nodded. He broke away from her and reached inside to pluck out a condom, then ripped it open with his teeth. He shucked his boxers, and when his cock sprang free, her eyes widened. With a chuckle, he fisted his length and gave a couple of lazy pumps.

She licked her lips, and not taking his eyes from those plump lips, he rolled the latex over his length. Then, grabbing her by the waist, Brett quickly, roughly flipped her over onto her stomach and pulled her hips up so that she knelt in front of him but kept her face in her pillow. With his knee, he nudged the inside of her smooth thigh, and she parted her legs obediently. He smiled and drew back his hand, bringing it across her ass with a loud slap. She jumped at the contact, and he smiled. He reached out and cupped her near-hairless pussy with his hand. He could feel her still-swollen flesh and her moisture on his fingers.

He resumed his position behind her, and without wasting any time, he pushed into her. He was rough, *too rough*, too demanding. But her groans of pleasure told him she needed this, too. He took everything from her that he wanted. But he didn't think that he would ever get enough. His fingers dug into her flesh and she fisted the blankets as his hips pistoned back and forth, in and out of her. She met each of his thrusts with a passion and ferocity that matched his own.

Through his loud grunts and groans, he could hear her cries. They were wild, barely human, just animals, and the only thing he could think about was bringing them both to release. He looked to his left and saw their reflection in the large mirror of her closet door. He saw each of his muscles tensing as he moved in and out of her, and he saw the arch of her back and the lines of her body. He watched in the mirror as he raised his hand and smacked her ass again. Rebecca screamed again, but she sped up her motions, bringing her hips back to meet his. He put a hand on her hip, another on her shoulder, and continued to drive into her. The hand on her hip dropped lower and to the front, and he found her clit. He spread her moisture around her, and he pulled her up so that her back, slick with sweat, was flush with his chest. Her cries were loud, growing louder by the second, and he knew she was close. He was, too. He kept pace until she stiffened in his arms and cried out her release, and then he let himself go. He came with a rush as his orgasm hit him, and he emptied inside her with a loud groan before they both tumbled onto the mattress.

Brett tried to catch his breath. "Fuck," he whispered. Being with Rebecca again was more incredible than he remembered. She was as beautiful as she'd been five years ago. He watched her splayed out next to him, coming down from her orgasm, and his mind flashed to that night in college when he'd talked about high school and his issues with addiction. Something had been freed within him that night, and he'd told her. But instead of making him feel at peace, it had opened him up to vulnerability. And vulnerability would be his downfall.

He didn't have time for analyzing his past, or the fact that after she'd gone off to New York, he'd been in the city and almost looked her up. But he hadn't. He had to focus on the present. And in the present, he had work to do.

The haze of his orgasm had cleared. Reality came crashing back. He'd had a moment of weakness, and now that his libido and his dick had been sufficiently taken care of, it was time to look after his livelihood. That was enough of a distraction. Thoughts of work overtook him as he remembered everything that was at stake. He tensed; he had to get out of there. He had to force her away from him. It was the only way.

He pushed himself up from the bed and disposed

of the condom in a nearby trash can. "That was great," he said, looking away from her, gathering his clothes. He pulled on his boxers and followed up with his pants. "Thanks."

"You're leaving?" she asked him, sitting up on the bed.

"Yeah, you didn't expect me to stick around and cuddle, did you?" he asked, buttoning his shirt.

She paused. Her eyebrows pinched together and a frown formed on her lips as she watched him get dressed. "I guess not."

"Becca—"

"Rebecca," she corrected him, a hard edge to her voice. She crossed her arms across her perfect breasts.

"Rebecca," he said. "Let's not make this any more than it is, okay? Why complicate things?" He looked away from her, because if he didn't, he knew he'd be gone. That he would slide back into bed with her. But he had to force himself to remember that he wasn't there to play nice. He wasn't her boyfriend. He'd gone back to her house to fulfill a biological urge, and *that was it*. They couldn't have whatever it was they'd had before. Not after everything that had happened between them.

Her smile was humorless. "No, you're right. This—whatever this is—shouldn't be any more complicated than it already is."

"It was fun, though, wasn't it? But I've got to

get back home. Get some sleep. I've got an early rise tomorrow."

"Fine. Go."

He hesitated, for just a moment. "Is this going to be a big deal?" he asked.

"No, of course not," she said, standing. She grasped her robe and put it on, tightening the belt. "It's just sex. Not like we haven't done it before." She shrugged and walked into the en suite bathroom. "You know your way out."

CHAPTER SEVEN

REBECCA POURED A mug of coffee and sat at the large table in the breakfast nook off the kitchen. Her father's house. He'd left it to her after his death, and while she'd redecorated some, the house still held much of her father's presence, like the old beat-up recliner that must have been over thirty years old. The brown leather was tattered, in need of repair, and in no way matched the gray furniture she'd bought, nor the yellow accents that brightened up the TV room. But she couldn't part with it. Nor could she move the reading glasses that he always seemed to fall asleep wearing while he watched the game or read the paper. They were still in their usual position on the end table near the right arm of the chair, easily within his reach.

Her father's absence caused an ache in her chest, and she knew that if he was still alive, he would know exactly how to deal with Collins/Fischer and the takeover bid. But he was gone. It was up to her, and she knew that she would be successful. It was her only option.

If only she could forget about her attraction to Brett and focus on the task at hand. She shook her head, reached for her coffee again and opened her laptop. She turned the computer on, and she was immediately greeted by her financial management program. She clicked over into the RMD page. Her original ownership in the company had grown in the past few days. She had finally dipped into the trust fund that she hadn't touched since she was twenty-one and started contacting shareholders on behalf of the secret holdings company that her father had created for her.

In order to keep Daniels International from the clutch of Brett's fingers and from falling under the umbrella of The Brotherhood, Rebecca had decided to use her own money to buy up shares in her own company. But she had to do it without Brett's knowing it was her. If he didn't know her plans, then he couldn't stop her. And it was working. She'd made a gain on shares of Daniels International, offering above Brett's asking price to people willing to sell them. Collins/Fischer still owned more than she did, but she'd managed to stall their progress by also offering a higher return on dividends in exchange. That would also cost her a pile of money, and she knew that her money manager probably wouldn't approve. But it was something she *had* to do to save the family business.

With two hands, she gripped the coffee mug and felt warmed by the heat of the sun pouring in through the huge glass panels that looked out onto the pool deck. With a wistful smile, she thought of Saturday mornings as a kid. When she'd wake up, and her father would already be at the table, reading the newspaper, but when he saw her, he would put it down and they would catch each other up on their lives. It was always her favorite part of the week. When it was just her and her father.

The peel of her cell phone ringing interrupted her thoughts. She picked it up and answered it, not recognizing the number on the caller ID. "Hello?"

"Rebecca?" the woman on the other end asked. "It's Alana."

Rebecca smiled. "Hey, how are you?"

"I'm great. I'm just calling to see if you'd like to have that brunch date. I'm free this afternoon, and if I don't get out of the house today, I'll just go to work. And I *need* a day off."

Rebecca thought about the stack of work she had to tackle that day, but she ignored it. She needed a day off, as well. "Yeah, sure. I'd love to." She looked at her watch. "I'll meet you in an hour."

Brett let himself into his parents' home. It was the house where he'd grown up, and while it was palatial, his parents still made it feel like a cozy home. While many of his well-off friends had been given free rein as teenagers, able to come and go, do as they pleased, Brett's parents had not given him such freedom. It was something he'd resented when he was younger, but he knew now that it just showed their mettle as parents. They'd remained interested in his life and goals—and problems—and it was partially the reason behind his rebellion. He'd been a stupid kid, craving the independence his friends had had, so he'd started sneaking out late, going to unsupervised parties in neighboring mansions, experimenting with substances. Kids with money could get their hands on anything. And he had. He'd gotten better and better at hiding his drug use, until it had exploded, and then his parents had been instrumental in his rehabilitation.

But no matter what problems he'd had or the trouble he'd caused, he'd never been a source of shame for his parents. They'd never shown him anything but unconditional love and support. That support was also what drove him to succeed on his own terms, to not want to succeed because of his surname or on anyone's terms but his own. It was why he was so determined to never lose or take his eyes off the prize. It drove his need to win at any cost.

He yawned, not having slept much; his Rebecca-caused insomnia might be the end of him. He was certain his eyes hadn't closed before the sun came up. His body still rigid with tension, anger, desire and a plethora of other emotions he couldn't identify. He walked into the kitchen. His father sat alone at the table, reading the paper, eating from a plate of scrambled eggs that Elaine, their incredible, long-serving housekeeper—more like a member of the family—had no doubt prepared before leaving for the day. Brett waved to his father, who looked up briefly, before he stopped at the stove and fixed himself a plate, which he piled high with bacon, eggs, toast and golden hash browns before going back for more bacon and coffee.

Brett took a seat across from his father, who looked up and put down the paper. Even though the man had every technological gadget on the market, he still opted to get his news from the morning paper. "Where's Mom?" Brett asked, buttering his slice of toast.

"She had a catering crisis for the benefit she's hosting for the animal shelter next weekend. You know how it goes. How important those animals are to her."

Brett laughed. "More important than us," he said, the joke that he and his father had shared for years. "Maybe this year she *won't* come home with an elderly rescue to let it live out its remaining years in comfort with you in your office."

"I don't believe that for a second. Those geriatric

animals are like her kryptonite. I don't know why she doesn't just stop with those functions. All the work that goes into them. She should be relaxing."

"And how exactly would you react if she told you to retire?" Brett asked, an eyebrow raised.

He looked at Brett over the rim of his glasses. "That's irrelevant."

Brett laughed and scooped a forkful of eggs into his mouth and chewed. "Sorry I'm late," he said.

"I was beginning to think I'd be eating alone. So what kept you?"

The fact that he hadn't been able to sleep for hours after leaving Rebecca's place had kept him. "Uh," he stammered. "I overslept this morning. I had kind of a long night."

"I know exactly what that means," his father responded. "Who's the woman?"

"What makes you think—" Brett stopped when his father shot him a pointed look. The man knew him too well. He smiled. He could never pull one over on his dad. "Old friend from college."

"Oh, that's nice. Getting back together, reminiscing, looking back on the good old days."

Brett laughed. "That wasn't exactly the type of relationship Rebecca and I had."

"Rebecca Daniels?"

"Yeah."

His father nodded in approval. "I had no idea that you were acquainted. She's back to run Daniels International, from what I hear. Her reputation precedes her. She's good, smart. Tough but nice. Are you seeing each other?"

The things he'd done with her the night before certainly hadn't been *nice*. Road head may have moved her over to the *naughty* column. But even less nice was the way they'd left things. Again. "Well, I wouldn't say we're *seeing each other…*"

His father watched him with shrewd eyes. "You say you overslept, but you look tired."

"Well, maybe I didn't get that much sleep," he admitted. "I was late getting home."

"And how was it?" his father asked casually, sipping from his coffee mug.

Brett almost choked on his eggs, and his eyes widened.

His father, catching on to his unintentional faux pas, coughed, as well. "I meant your night. In general. Without any gory details, please."

"It was fine."

"Especially seeing as how you're trying to take over her company."

Brett blew out a frustrated breath and drank from his coffee. Not much happened in Las Vegas without Garrett Collins hearing about it. "How'd you know about that?"

His father smirked but said nothing. Brett rolled his eyes, knowing that the business community in Las Vegas was small, and the old stodgy men who ruled it gossiped more than a little old ladies' sew-ing circle. "Tell me what's really behind your move on Daniels."

"It's just part of a move to dismantle our com-petition. It's survival of the fittest in this world. We want to be the only real estate game in town. It happens all the time. You've done it yourself."

"Yes, but never involving the company of a woman I'm sleeping with." His father put his el-bows on the table and leaned closer to Brett. "So care to share why you're doing it?"

"It's business," Brett snapped. "Jesus, why do I have to answer for it at every turn?"

"I'm only asking because so far, you and Alex have been very deliberate in your actions, only act-ing when you're sure it's the right move. But this takeover is extremely sudden and a very serious matter. So I'm curious. Why now? Why so sud-den?"

Brett thought about sticking with the *it's busi-ness* mantra he'd been saying all along, but he knew he wouldn't fool his father. He looked down at his plate and picked at his food.

"Brett?"

"We've always had this back-and-forth ani-mosity, a competition, but we really connected, too, you know? Physically," he added. "Rebecca does something to me, and she's a distraction I don't need." Suddenly, Brett found himself telling his dad everything—about his relationship with Rebecca in college, about the night he'd told her about his past when so few people knew. About the way she made him lose focus and feel out of control. It felt good to let it out, and his dad listened without judgment. "If her company folds, then there's no reason for her to stick around. At this point, we're so far deep into this that only one of us can survive." It was true, even if he wanted to take it all back, he couldn't now—a complete turnaround of his actions would raise questions about his conviction and reflect badly on his reputation in the business world. "And now Alex is skeptical of me and my motives, as he should be. I just don't know what to do." Brett hated admitting to anyone, especially his father, his lack of control.

"Pride's a hell of a thing, isn't it?" Garrett commented. "I could see how hard it was for you to say that. You always have such a firm grasp on your life, so methodical and in control. And I know that's because of what happened when you were younger."

His addiction.

"You told her about your problems with drugs?"

"Yeah. We were hanging out one night, and the floodgates gave way, and I told her everything. She shared some things with me, as well. At that moment, I'd felt closer to anyone than I ever had. I didn't feel like so much of a screwup."

His father nodded. "You're a good man, Brett.

Sure, you had a rocky start, but your mother and I—and all your friends and partners—are proud of you. I might have helped you guys out and given you a small edge very early in your career. But everything you have now is because you worked your ass off for it. Don't forget that."

Brett nodded, not sure how much he believed him. "Thanks. But until we're the biggest name in town, I won't be able to prove it."

They sat in silence, each of them stewing over the conversation.

But then the poignant silence was over. "I'm guessing you're close to being a majority stakeholder of Daniels International?" his father asked, thankfully bringing the conversation back to a topic that they were both comfortable with—the business.

"We're at over twenty percent. But Rebecca has gotten to many shareholders and they're reluctant to sell. We bought up a lot of the odds and ends, and only a few remain. With the exception of what's owned by Collins/Fischer, there's also a substantial amount owned by a company called RMD. Have you ever heard of them?"

His father thought about it. "No. Never heard of them. Maybe they're not local."

"Maybe," Brett muttered. His mind was no longer on brunch or conversing with his father. His thoughts ran back to Rebecca, RMD and just what the hell he was doing.

* * *

Rebecca sipped from her mimosa, grateful for the cool beverage as she sat on the terrace of the restaurant that Alana had suggested. The sun shone down, and even though it was before noon, the temperature was in the high eighties, so she sipped again, willing her internal temperature to cool. The drink was delicious, refreshing, *strong*, definitely made with the good stuff. She checked her watch and saw that Alana was a couple of minutes late, and Rebecca feared she would finish her drink and have to order another one before Alana got there. She'd given herself extra time to get there when she'd realized she'd have to cab back to Thalia and pick up her car before driving here.

Around her, people happily brunched. The restaurant was packed and there was a lineup for an outside table on the terrace, but all she'd had to do was mention that she was meeting Alana and she was seated at a somehow-empty table. It seemed that The Brotherhood's influence was well-known.

She'd nearly drained her champagne flute as Alana bustled in. She was polished, gorgeous, glossed and well dressed. Alana always had an immaculate sense of style, and Rebecca had never seen her anything less than put together. But that morning, she was flustered, hurried.

"I'm so sorry I'm late," she said, taking a seat opposite Rebecca. "Traffic was a nightmare. I don't know what I was thinking, taking the Strip. It was typically awful. I think I used my middle finger so many times I sprained it."

"I've been gone for years, and even I know you don't drive on the Strip," she said with a laugh. "Don't worry about it," Rebecca said, finishing the mimosa. She felt the alcohol hit her empty stomach. "Although, we'd better order some food before I have another one of these on an empty stomach."

"Good idea," Alana said, gesturing to the waiter for a drink. "I'm glad we could get together."

"Me, too. I've been here for six months, but I'm pretty sure I've only managed to spend time at home and at the office."

"Don't forget the club. Di Terrestres," Alana said with a raised, sharply manicured eyebrow. "And your dinner last night. Except I heard from my guys that you and Brett didn't exactly stay for dinner."

Rebecca opened her mouth, but she didn't speak. She didn't even know how to respond. "Oh, look! Our drinks are here!" Rebecca said instead, as the server brought them glasses on a silver serving tray.

They toasted and drank. And Rebecca looked across the table at her old friend. "Tell me about your life. What's new with you? Are you seeing anyone?"

Alana laughed. "No. Dating hasn't been going well. A lot of guys are afraid of a woman who can take care of herself. There hasn't been anyone in my life for a while, outside of some casual flings. I tried the online apps and all that. But I deleted them all after the last guy I matched with told me he believed that the female orgasm was a myth. So, you can see how well that went."

"You're kidding!" Rebecca guffawed. "I'll bet that poor fool has never pleasured a woman in his life."

"Hand to God. He said it something like, *the feminists* made it up to make men feel bad about themselves."

"Tell me you didn't give him a chance to prove him wrong."

"I absolutely did not. In fact, I ended the night alone in my bed proving to *myself* how wrong he was."

They shared a laugh while they sipped their drinks, but soon, the laughter died and left them in a poignant silence. Rebecca felt Alana watching her, scrutinizing. "What?"

"You're so keen to ask about me, but really I'm curious about what's going on with you and Brett."

She knew the question was coming. And she didn't have a straightforward response. "The easy answer is I have no idea." She shrugged. "The man is trying to take over my company. And there's no way in hell I'm going to let him." She drank more from her glass. "And he's so frustrating and arrogant and smug. But goddammit, the minute he looks at me, I just feel my panties slip off on their own." Rebecca remembered that the woman sitting across from her was one of Brett's best friends and business partners. "Oh, my God. I'm sorry. I shouldn't have said that."

Alana waved her off. "Don't worry about it. The way the guys talk about sex, especially since we've opened the club, that's nothing shocking to me. I know that you guys had a bit of a rivalry, a war since you got back to the city."

"Yeah, and he went full nuclear."

"But you're still sleeping together?"

Rebecca thought back to the way Brett had left her house the night before. "Well, we're not exactly *sleeping together*." Rebecca laughed without answering, falling back into a pleasant groove with her old friend.

"He's been kind of tense lately."

Wanting to change the topic from how *tense* Brett was and their relationship, Rebecca looked around. "You sure did get us a good table. All I had to do was drop your name."

"Oh, yeah," Alana said without much enthusiasm. "My male partners in the good ol' boys' club get all the great business connections, but I get the nice tables."

"That's always the way, though, isn't it? It doesn't matter what we do or how successful we are, if a man is doing it, too, we might as well be in the kitchen making them sandwiches."

"You're telling me. I may co-own and run some of the hottest restaurants and clubs in the city, but I have to name-drop my friends to get people to take me seriously."

"Is that why you're all named The Brotherhood?" Rebecca asked with a mysterious tone.

"Ha!" Alana laughed once. "You know about that foolishness?"

"Yeah, but Brett said the name was your idea."

"Yeah, I made it up, ironically, because they're all such big important tough guys," she said with a dramatic eye roll. "But it stuck, and now they just use that name to annoy me. I'm certain of it. Guess that's who they are. Pests, the lot of them. But they're all good guys, and we're more family than friends. I missed having a girlfriend in the city, though," she said, reaching across the table to cup her hand over Rebecca's. The waiter came to the table, and they both ordered crepes with fruit, chocolate and whipped cream, and, of course, another round of mimosas.

When the server left, Rebecca smiled and clinked her glass against Alana's again. "Hear, hear. I didn't really have a lot of friends in New York. I was just so focused on work. I dated a few guys here and there, thanks to the internet. But it's hard to make friends when you're a grown-up."

"You're telling me." Alana laughed. "I'm in desperate need of some female company. My only friends sometimes act as if they forget I have breasts."

Rebecca laughed. "How do you do it? How do you work with those guys? God, you can just smell the testosterone when they walk into a room."

Alana laughed and sipped from her glass and leaned over the table, bringing her face closer to Rebecca's. "I'm going to let you in on a secret. They're so busy strutting their stuff and showing off their feathers, they don't realize that I'm actually running all of this."

Rebecca almost spit out her mimosa, but she swallowed and looked at the other woman in awe. "Behind every successful man there's an even more badass woman."

"You're goddamn right there is," Alana agreed.

Rebecca took a deep breath. Alana's words of wisdom gave her a newfound hope, strength. She could persevere. She could beat Brett. It was possible. She was a *badass woman*. "Yeah," she said with a smile as she looked at the powerful, successful woman who sat across from her at the table. They were allies in a way, but what was more important, she felt she could count on Alana to be her friend going forward.

"It's no secret that you and Brett were hooking

up when we were in college, even though you could barely stand each other."

"Yeah, if there was anything we had in common, it was sex and fighting." Rebecca thought about it. "I guess some things never change."

"What happened to make him want to buy you out? I don't believe that it's strictly business. Something about this is affecting him more than I've seen. He doesn't take kindly to people messing with The Brotherhood's business dealings."

"I was hoping you could give me a little insight on that one. Sure, I beat them in a deal, they screwed with one of my suppliers, and then one of their employees came to work for DI," Rebecca said, listing through her recent rivalry with Collins/Fischer. "I just don't know why he's gone so far with it."

"He's stubborn, and when he sets his sights on something, he goes for it. But he doesn't get that there are more important things in life than the job. I don't know how to call him off. I wish I could help."

"No, that's okay. I'll figure it out. I have some tricks up my sleeve that he doesn't know about."

"How are you fighting it? Think you can hold on to enough of the shares?"

Rebecca straightened in her seat, eyed Alana warily and was immediately suspicious that there was an ulterior motive to today's brunch. Was Alana just another head-on attack from The Brotherhood, to dig up information, distract her and loosen her grip on her company?

Alana raised her fingers to her mouth. "Oh, God, I'm sorry, I can't believe I was so intrusive. Forget I asked. I'm just used to talking like that with the guys. It's always blunt shoptalk and strategy."

"It's fine," Rebecca told her, still maintaining a distance. She'd trusted Alana back in college and felt she still could. And she wanted a friend, but she would have to remember to be careful around all of them. Anything she said could easily make its way back to Brett.

"Listen, I mean this," Alana said. "Brett is one of my business partners and closest friends, but I am here with you as a friend. I know how isolating the business world can be sometimes, especially as a woman. But I'm here to talk if you need it. God knows that I do sometimes."

"Thanks," Rebecca said, reaching across the table, putting her hand over Alana's. Rebecca smiled, glad to finally be able to relax and build a new relationship and have a new start. Maybe that was what she needed in every aspect of her life. She didn't have a lot of time to think about it because the waiter arrived, carrying their food. And for one afternoon, Rebecca could forget about the business, the past, and just focus on being a woman with no other worries than the fat content of her brunch.

CHAPTER EIGHT

BRETT'S HOME WAS his refuge. And while he'd designed it to his specifications, he didn't spend nearly enough time there. But even when he was home, he couldn't exactly turn off work. There was always something to do, something that needed his attention. And with the extra work he'd taken on with the takeover of Daniels International, he had so much more to do.

He sat at his desk, staring at the stacks of paperwork, contracts, bids, all the things he'd let pile up that week, while he had focused on the Daniels International acquisition. He was always so good at multitasking, but Rebecca had thrown him off his focus. He had to get his head on straight. So, every time his phone beeped, the announcement of yet another email that needed his attention, he exhaled and took a gulp of his long-cold coffee, then turned back to his work and tried to focus in quiet.

The quiet was short-lived, however, when his doorbell rang. He looked up, not used to the sound or even having people in his home. He furrowed his eyebrows and considered ignoring it. He didn't have time for anyone selling magazine subscriptions or passing out religious tracts, so he tried to go back to his work. But the bell rang again.

Frustrated, his patience tested, he threw down the contract he was studying and stood. He stomped down the stairs to his front door and pulled back the door. "What?" he yelled before seeing who was standing on the other side. But seeing Rebecca outside his door did nothing to ease his tension.

He looked at her. He was tired, and just one look at her made him want her, and he didn't have the energy to fight the desire. He cursed his own lack of control. "What are you doing here?"

She looked him dead in the eye. "We need to talk. And actually talk this time."

"I don't think we do."

"Come on, Brett. Too afraid to have a conversation?" she challenged.

"Not afraid, just not interested. I don't think we have anything to discuss."

"For fuck's sake." Rebecca sighed. "Just let me in."

Brett stepped aside, and she pushed past him. "What do you want to discuss?"

"I had brunch with Alana today."

"Okay."

"And it might have just been talking it out with

another woman or the bottomless mimosas, but I'm so sick of this, Brett." She stuck out her hand. "Hi, I'm Rebecca Daniels."

Brett looked at her hand. "What are you doing?"

She didn't waver under his stare. The one that made powerful men cower. "It's nice to meet you," she said.

"Rebecca." He sighed. "I'm too tired for this."

"So am I. Since day one we've hated each other, we were a threat to one another. But we're adults now, and we're still playing the same games for power and dominance. Brett, we need to start over before someone gets hurt."

"It's too late for that."

"I don't think it is. Why don't we just forget the past, forget all the ways we've screwed each other over?"

"I'm not pulling back from the buyout. I've got my own partners and shareholders to think about."

"I know you won't be. And I wouldn't expect you to. In regard to the takeover, why don't we just see where that goes and let the better company win?"

Rebecca still stood in front of him with her hand extended. She was right of course. He knew that he didn't have time for games anymore. There wasn't enough time or energy for him to do everything he wanted, and if he could put whatever was happening between him and Rebecca in its own little box, it would make his life a lot easier. He would own her company by the end of the week of course, but it didn't mean that they couldn't be civil until then. Something in him let go, and he smiled down at her. He took her hand in his and shook. "Hi, I'm Brett."

"So we can forget about all the crap and just be regular people and leave all of the takeover stuff in the boardroom?"

"I'd like that."

He cupped his palm over her shoulder, her delicate skin left exposed by her sleeveless blouse. He dragged his hand downward, sliding over her skin. He could feel her muscles flex and tense under his touch. He couldn't help but think that things could have easily been different with Rebecca. "I'm sorry it's worked out like this."

"Me, too."

"I was just about to make some dinner. Why don't you stay and join me? You know, to make up for the one we didn't eat the other night?"

Her breath was a shudder as the air left her body. And he grinned at her, taking another step closer so that they were only a whisper apart, her breasts pressed against his chest.

"I should leave."

He ducked his head and skimmed his lips over the outer shell of her ear. "Yeah, probably. But you won't."

She blinked, and he knew from experience that her restraint was wire thin. Just like his. She blinked and looked around his home, and he knew it was to distract herself, to not relent to him.

"This is a pretty nice place," she managed to say before he couldn't take it any longer and his lips slammed down on hers. He walked her back until she was pressed into the wall, trapped between it and his chest. He wrapped her delicate wrists in his hands and pushed to the wall, above her head.

"I'll give you the tour later," he said against her lips before taking them again. Her lips parted and he took great advantage, plunging his tongue inside her mouth. It found hers and twined with it, stroking, tasting. Her flavor was one that he'd deprived himself of for over five years, and in the past few days, he'd drank from her like a man who'd survived a drought. He might have control over his past dependence on drugs and alcohol, but it was Rebecca who was his addiction, and he would always need his fix. If he'd learned anything, it was that there was no rehab for that.

He took her hand and practically dragged her up the stairs to his bedroom. He couldn't wait another second. They stood at the foot of his king-size bed, kissing, tearing, ripping at each other's clothing. She lifted his shirt, and he pulled away only long enough to pull it over his head and throw it behind him. He reached around her and, finding the zipper at the back of her blouse, he pulled it down. It snagged briefly on the material, and he yanked it impatiently, pulling it too hard. He felt the fabric tear. He'd have to buy her a new top in the morning. He would buy her a thousand blouses or keep her in his home naked. He didn't care. He let the ruined fabric fall to the floor with a light swoosh, and she pulled down her skirt and stood before him in her bra and panties.

He stood back a little, to get a look at her. "Christ, Rebecca," he muttered. "You're so fucking beautiful. There are so many things I want to do with you. The last two times, it wasn't close to enough." He shook his head. "I have no idea where to start."

She reached back and unclasped her bra and let the lacy material fall to the floor. "Start here."

CHAPTER NINE

WHEN BRETT TOOK a step back from her, Rebecca saw his eyes roam over her body as she stood before him in her pale blue satin panties and her black high-heel shoes. The dark, wild look in his eyes made her feel more like an animal's prey than a woman, and a low growl emitted from his throat and exited from his parted lips. He took a predatory step toward her again, wrapping his arms around her waist and lifted her, not taking his eyes from hers. And he lowered her onto the center of his massive bed.

She was mostly naked, but Brett still had half his clothes on. If he had any idea what a specimen of masculinity he was, he never let on, because he only watched her, and she felt like the center of his world. His hands went to his belt, where those oh-so-skilled fingers tackled the buckle and whipped the strip of leather from the loops at his waist with a quick swish. With a quick flick of his fingers, the button was undone and he lowered the zipper and pushed his jeans from his hips until they fell at his feet.

Watching him from her place on the bed, her eyelids at half-mast with desire, she took in his body. He was a beautiful, powerful man. More muscular than he'd been eleven years ago, with more hair covering him than before. She couldn't wait to ball her fists in the dark hair that covered his pecs and trailed down in a neat line that continued past the band of his tight boxers, which were appreciably tented with his erection. They'd been naked together many times, and recently at that, but that didn't stop her from marveling at his body. He hooked his thumbs under the elastic waistband, and she held her breath as he dragged his shorts down, past the pronounced V of his hips, the veins that ran underneath his belly button to his groin. She caught a glimpse of well-groomed hair, and she was riveted, unable to pull her eyes away. But he paused, his hands frozen just as they were about to reveal his rigid length. She looked back to his face, and saw that he was watching her, a playful smile playing on his lips.

Instead of completely disrobing, he joined her on the bed. "I've wanted to be with you again for so long, Rebecca," he murmured as he knelt over her on the massive king-size bed. "The past week has definitely proved that you can go home again."

Rebecca looked up at him. "Then what are you waiting for?"

A wicked smile crossed his lips, and his body covered hers. His warmth burned her as her arms encircled his neck and pulled him closer, until he was pressed against her. He grasped her wrists in his large hands and pushed them against the mattress on either side of her head. She was his captive, and she had no problem with that. She would stay bound by him forever if he wanted.

He kissed her long, hard, his lips playing hers, demanding her acquiescence, and she surrendered to him. Holding her wrists in place, he palmed her breast as his lips and teeth descended over the stiff bud of her nipple. He nibbled on her lightly, and she arched her back toward him, causing her chest to crush into his face. He didn't complain. He released his grip on her wrists, focusing all his attention on her breasts. He feasted on her. His mouth deliciously tortured one breast while his fingers played on the other, caressing, squeezing, nipping.

The way he played her body, the way he brought her so close to the edge only stimulating her breasts, was something she hadn't experienced before. She had never been so sensitive, and she was torn between pulling him closer and pushing him away to keep breathing. He was a master of her body.

His touch moved lower as he dragged his lips and his fingertips down her torso, until they found their rightful place at the band of her lace panties. She was glad she'd carefully chosen her lingerie when she'd dressed earlier today.

He hummed in appreciation as he hooked his thumbs underneath the band. Slowly—torturously so—he dragged them down over her hips, and she aided him by lifting them off the bed. He looked up at her, and a wolfish smile played on his lips. He looked like a man who was about to take everything he wanted and, *goddamn*, Rebecca threw her head back onto a pillow that smelled like Brett and closed her eyes as he pulled her panties over her ankles and his mouth descended onto her pussy.

The minute he touched her, his tongue sliding along her wet, needy crevice, the scream that pealed from her lips and rang through the room shocked her. It felt like years since she'd been touched, tasted like Brett was doing now as his tongue and lips found all her most sensitive spots. And she supposed it had been. No one she'd been with since Brett had affected her in such a way, making her desperate, making her shake with need. His lips closed over her clit, and the bundle of nerves was grateful for the attention. But she needed more. She could feel his cock, hard against her leg, as his mouth drove her wild with need.

As his mouth worked diligently, he thrust a finger inside her, then another. It was close, but not what she needed. But she was already so far gone with his mouth and fingers, she found herself perched at the edge of pleasure. With his other hand, Brett grasped her ass, one of his fingers intentionally skirting the sensitive puckering, and she felt herself being thrust over the cliff, raptured with pleasure. She cried out and grabbed the back of Brett's head, pulling at his hair. Not that he needed to be persuaded to stay of course, because he stayed with her for every glorious beat, licking, touching softly as her thunderous orgasm washed over her.

When she could breathe again, Rebecca released her grip on Brett's hair, and he rose up over her. He covered her again, his lips tracing her jawline, grazing over her earlobe. "Fuck, you taste so goddamn good," he said roughly before taking her lips in another scorching kiss. She could taste herself on his lips and tongue. And it was a highly erotic sense that made her want more, more of him, more of her, more of them.

Brett moaned into her mouth and pulled away abruptly. "It's gotta be now, Becca. I can't wait another second." He rolled away from her to the edge of the huge bed. He reached into his bedside table and withdrew a square foil packet. He tossed it on the bed and returned to her, knelt above her. Her legs were spread wantonly, bracketing his thighs, and she watched, riveted, as he finally lowered his short designer boxers. His rigid length sprang out, long and hard, from a neat cloud of dark curls.

Her eyes hooded from her orgasm, she watched him as he grasped his dick in his fist and gave a couple of languid pumps before rolling the latex over himself. Still kneeling, he reached for her, grabbing her waist, and he lifted her, pulling her to him as her legs locked around his hips so they lined up perfectly. With just the subtlest of movements, she felt Brett position himself at her core, and with one solid thrust he was inside her.

He pulled back his hips a little and then thrust back into her. She came to and found her rhythm, meeting him thrust for thrust. He grunted in her ear, a rough sound, wild, but it did something to her. It turned her on. And she moved frantically, smacking her hips against his, increasing her pace, trying to take control, but she knew it wouldn't last for long.

Brett slammed her back down to the mattress and lay on top of her. His pace quickened as he thrust inside her, his hips pumping wildly, driving his cock into her at a blinding pace. She could barely catch her breath as he brought her to higher and higher peaks of pleasure, until she felt herself flying as another orgasm took her over. She cried out Brett's name, her nails driving into the skin of his broad shoulders. His groan was loud, and she felt him stiffen above her before he exhaled. Then his body loosened, and he rolled off her and landed heavily beside her.

* * *

Brett disengaged from Rebecca and disposed of the used condom before rolling back onto the bed. He was spent, but he was ready to go again. He would always have enough energy for Rebecca. He threw his forearm over his eyes and attempted to regain his breath. He felt her breathing beside him on the mattress. God. Being with her again—being inside her—was more incredible than he ever could have imagined, better than he remembered from his college days. And more amazing than sex had been with any other woman he'd been with in years.

He turned his head and watched her. She was on her back; her lips were parted as she pulled needed air into her body. Her eyes were wide, and he wondered what she was thinking about. He heard her sigh, and she looked back at him. "Wow," she whispered.

"You're telling me."

Brett felt his empty stomach demand his attention and he remembered that he'd offered her dinner, and he was starving. "Still up for that dinner?"

"I'm starving. What do you have in mind?" she asked him.

He had a few things on his mind. But his empty stomach protested. "I'm going to cook you something. My mom would be horrified about what a poor host I've become."

"You'd be the shame of the society pages." Rebecca laughed and rolled over onto her stomach, propping herself up on her elbows. "So what are you making me for dinner?"

CHAPTER TEN

REBECCA, DRESSED ONLY in Brett's white shirt, walked barefoot to the kitchen, where he was putting the finishing touches on what smelled like an incredible meal of spaghetti. Hours had passed since she'd shown up at his home, ready for confrontation, and after her several vigorous "workouts" with Brett, she was starving.

He was shirtless, wearing only a pair of pale gray low-slung lounging pants that exposed the defined V of his hip bones and the trail of dark hair that disappeared behind the drawstring waist. He stood at the stove. The broad expanse of his back and shoulders rippled as he moved over the stovetop, stirring, adding ingredients, tasting. Even watching Brett cook was sexy. Everything he did was sexy.

He turned around and, seeing her, smiled and handed her a glass of red wine that he'd poured for her. She sipped and saw that he did the same from a tall glass of soda water. They made eye contact over the rims of their glasses, and his eyes crinkled at the corners, twinkling. He was smiling at her. Since she'd come to his place that afternoon, it was as if they'd reached some sort of understanding. They'd cleared the air about their past when they'd reintroduced themselves. They still had a great deal to hash out regarding their current business dealings, but they could deal with that later. She needed just a few hours of relaxation, when that wasn't at the forefront of her mind. She wanted to enjoy the easy camaraderie she'd found with Brett. At least for the night.

The wine was good. She knew she should expect only the best. "If you're sober, why do you keep wine in your house?"

"For guests," he explained with a shrug. "I entertain from time to time."

"So do you mind that I'm drinking this?"

"No, don't be ridiculous. Just because I don't drink, it doesn't mean that I expect everyone around me to abstain, as well. Addiction is my ongoing issue, no one else's. I wouldn't put that on my friends and family."

"You really haven't had anything to drink in twelve years?" she asked him carefully.

He shook his head and turned back to the stove. "Not one drink. No weed, no cocaine, no pills. I'm living clean these days. Except for caffeine. I will always need that fix." He chuckled.

"No other vices?" she asked with a raised eyebrow.

"Just one," he told her, looking over his shoulder, his voice as dark as his eyes. "There's sex."

She tried to ignore the heat in his eyes in favor of her growling stomach; at this rate, she'd never get food. And a girl had to eat. "Is dinner ready yet?"

"Let's eat."

Brett brought their plates to where Rebecca sat at the table. It surprised him how well she fit into his home, his life. He'd never had a woman there before. It had been years since he'd even considered having a relationship with a woman, and he never brought his one-night stands to his home. It was his territory. She was wearing his shirt, and it looked goddamn good on her.

She twirled some of the pasta onto her fork and brought it to her mouth. She tasted it and chewed, then moaned with pleasure. When she swallowed, she sipped her wine. "That's so good. Where did you learn to cook?"

"After we opened Thalia—that was The Brotherhood's first restaurant—we all had some informal private lessons with the head chef whom Alana had hired."

"Like I said the other night, I've heard great things about Thalia," she told him.

"Yeah, we should definitely go back there some night, and actually eat there."

"Oh, I don't know, we almost *ate* there last time," she said with a smirk before sipping her wine.

Brett coughed in surprise at her double entendre and drank water to clear his throat. He laughed. "Yeah, I guess we did."

"How many restaurants do you guys own?"

"We have four," he explained. "Alana runs those and Di Terrestres, and she designed them. Some of the most profitable business in The Brotherhood are her babies. It's a group effort. We all have a part in it. The restaurants and the club. And then there's Collins/Fischer and all the real estate, the office buildings, the condos. And we oversee several charities, as well."

Rebecca was impressed. "You guys have built quite the little empire, it seems."

"Well, we get by."

"Clearly."

"That's good," she said and, after taking another forkful of spaghetti, moaned again in satisfaction.

"You like it?"

She swallowed. "It's so good. I can't believe that you're so domestic."

"I've changed a lot in the last five years." He watched her. "You have, too."

"Yeah, I guess you're right."

"Before you came in here yelling at me a couple

of hours ago, how was your lunch with Alana?" he asked after several beats of silence had passed.

"It was great," she said. "We had too many mimosas and a fantastic conversation."

"Girl talk, eh?" he asked. "Did you talk about me?"

"Your name might have come up."

"I'm afraid to ask."

"It was somewhat complimentary, I assure you," she replied with a grin. "What did you do today?"

"I had brunch with my dad. I go over there every other week. We catch up over scrambled eggs and pastry."

"That's nice. How are your parents?"

"They're great. Still very active. Dad still spends most of his time at the office, and Mom stays busy with her charities."

They ate in silence again. "Brett, I think we need to address the elephant in the room," she said abruptly, putting down her fork and looking at him. She straightened her shoulders.

"Okay, what would you like to say?" Her sudden seriousness when they'd fallen into light and casual conversation took him by surprise. But he faced her head-on, trying to emanate that he was also in "business mode."

"I'm asking you again. I know we agreed to let it play out, but I want you to abandon your takeover bid."

He'd almost let his guard down. As she sat at his table, enjoying food he'd made for her, he'd forgotten about everything that stood between them. Had she actually been enjoying herself a few moments ago, or was she working up to this all along? "Do you now?" he said gruffly. "I don't see that happening. When I want something, I go for it. I'm sorry if that upsets you, but it's business."

"I'm not upset, because I'm going to win." They ate a few bites in silence before Brett heard his cell phone ring. "I should get that," he told her.

"Go right ahead," she told him without looking up from her plate.

He stood and tried to locate the sound and realized that he had left it in the kitchen.

Still within view of Rebecca, Brett found his phone and checked the caller ID before answering. It was Alex. "Yeah?"

"Hey, man, I hope I'm not interrupting anything."

He cast a look at Rebecca. She was eating and sipping her wine, not paying him any attention. "No, I can talk," he said.

"Is Rebecca there?"

"Maybe."

"So I *am* interrupting."

"You're about an hour past interrupting anything really important," he said. "So why are you calling?"

"Maybe I just want to hear the sound of your

voice," Alex wisecracked. "No, really, though, it's RMD. Their stake in Daniels has jumped to thirty percent. It's not a coincidence. There's no doubt they're making a play for Daniels stock. I was just talking to our private investigator, and he's got a little bit of info on RMD."

Brett stiffened. "And?"

"Not much so far. We don't know much about them, but they were established around nine years ago. And they held only ten percent for that long until we put out our tender offer. Now they've been going hard getting their own shares. I could even track their purchases as those from people we've already approached. They're buying the shares we need for our own takeover."

"So who is RMD?" he blurted out. "Do we know anything yet?" He caught Rebecca's eyes as they snapped to attention, meeting his own. He slipped quietly into his bedroom, giving himself more privacy. The sheets and pillows were still rumpled, and his room smelled like Rebecca. The floral essence of her skin permeated everything and overpowered the smell of pure animal sex.

"There's no indication," Alex said. "I can't find any info on these guys anywhere. Besides the fact that for years they'd held only ten percent, and in recent weeks their shares have tripled."

"Fuck. It's just a hurdle we didn't anticipate. We

just need to figure out who these guys are and stop them from acquiring any more shares."

"Want to get together tomorrow for lunch and come up with a plan?"

"Sounds good, man. Text me when and where. Thanks for calling." Brett disconnected and walked out of his bedroom to find himself face-to-face with Rebecca. "Hey," he said, narrowing his eyes at her. "Everything all right?"

Her eyes were wide. "Yeah, I'm fine. I was just on my way to the bathroom."

He watched her. Suspicion narrowed his eyebrows, but instead he smiled. "It's just down there," he said, pointing in the direction of the bathroom.

"Thanks," she said, quickly moving past him. He tried not to focus on her ass as she disappeared behind the door. His eyes narrowed again. Rebecca had followed him to the bedroom. To spy on him, to listen in on his end of the phone call.

Is that why she's here? His eyes narrowed at the closed bathroom door. Had she come here today to form a truce of sorts, or was this all part of her plan to fight back and keep her company? Shit. If that's all it took for him to slip up, he really did need this woman gone.

And if she thought she could come over here and have sex with him to get her way, she had another think coming. He opened the messaging app on his phone and dashed off a few words to the concierge at Di Terrestres. What he had planned for Rebecca would make her wish she'd never played this kind of game with him.

CHAPTER ELEVEN

REBECCA SAT BEHIND her desk, and with a red marker, she crossed off another name. One by one, she was scooping up shares in Daniels International. It was her only way to secure power and keep it away from Brett or anyone else who might try to wrestle it from her hands. She smiled, satisfied. She'd already acquired nearly a third of the shares, including those shares her father had given her when she was younger, and what she inherited. Hopefully, it would be enough to hold Brett at bay, and make her a majority shareholder.

The man whose name she'd just crossed off had accepted the offer she'd sent to buy his shares of the company. That put her in direct competition with Brett and Alex. Just a few more and she'd be done. The huge weight on her shoulders was lightening, the noose loosening, and she smiled again. Nothing could spoil her mood. She had been working her ass off, and soon it would pay off. She would soon own enough shares in Daniels International that she wouldn't have to worry about losing it ever again. Her dreams were just a breath away from being a reality. But it wasn't a guarantee yet.

The shareholders' annual meeting was scheduled for the upcoming Friday. In only five days, she would drop the bomb on Brett and the rest of the board that she was majority owner. Or she would be, once she secured those shares belonging to the few stragglers who hadn't committed either way. She just had to make it to Friday and get to them before Brett did. She frowned, remembering the look on his face when he'd caught her trying to listen in on his phone call. And how his attitude had changed once she'd exited the bathroom. The easy rapport they'd established had been broken, and she'd left not long after. He knew about RMD, and he had to know that she was up to something. It was only a matter of time before he put the pieces together.

Her office door was open and she looked past it, seeing a deliveryman exit the elevator and come onto the floor. He was carrying a huge bouquet of tropical flowers. She went back to her work, indifferent to his presence, and she was surprised when he stopped outside the door to stand in front of her assistant's desk.

Amy stood and came to her door. "Ms. Daniels," she started, a bright smile on her face. "There's a delivery for you. I already signed for it."

"Okay, thanks," she said, welcoming the deliveryman into her office. He crossed the floor and plonked the huge bouquet down on her desk.

The flowers were beautiful, but they took up a huge portion of the surface of her desk. What was she supposed to do with them while she worked? She picked through the buds and eventually found the card. And she smiled when she saw the inscription. *Rebecca, thanks for last night. Meet me tonight at Di Terrestres. Eight o'clock.*

It wasn't signed. But there was absolutely no doubt whom it was from. And she knew that he wasn't asking her to join him. It was an order. She cocked her head to the side and looked at the flowers. Maybe Brett wasn't so mad after all.

"Okay, dude, walk me through this," Alex told Brett. They were having lunch at Thalia when Brett had let him in on his plans for later that evening. "You're doing what?"

"I'm going to take Rebecca down to one of the exhibition rooms," Brett said. "I'm going to turn this around on her. Make her weak, make her beg, and then I'll show her that I'm in charge, and there's no way she can take me down."

"But why?" Alex asked. "I don't know how this helps us professionally—it's starting to sound like wounded pride is running things here. She's beating us, and you're desperate."

Brett bristled at his friend's accusation, no matter how true the words might be. He wasn't sure why he'd framed it as a business move—perhaps what he really needed was a friend right now, and Alex was that. He might have been desperate. But the desperation wasn't just to win, it was for Rebecca. The pure crush of desire and wanting leveled him, so he felt it was difficult to think of anything but being with her again. He cursed his weakness and lack of focus.

"That isn't what's happening." Brett said it forcefully, but Alex knew him better than he knew himself. He *did* have a score to settle with Rebecca. She'd managed to pull his focus. And it made him madder than hell, especially when she seemed so capable of keeping her head in the game. "Besides, she's definitely up to something. We were together the other night. We'd made amends and decided to just forget the business for a little while, but you have no idea how easily she came back around to the subject of the takeover. And then she was listening in on our phone call. If she's using sex against me, I need to, too. She's bounced back from our bid stronger than we thought, but sex has always been the way we get to each other. I know I can make her vulnerable this way." Brett folded his arms stubbornly across his chest.

"I don't know." Alex sighed. "Isn't it risky, taking her down there? It's not like the rest of the club.

Not just anyone can go down there. What if she leaks what happens there? Sure, she's seen the main room, but downstairs is another world."

Brett didn't respond. The exhibition rooms were the secret of Di Terrestres, not open to the general population—just their VIP clientele, who were looking for some more immersive, erotic pursuits. The takeover might have been on his mind, but it was grossly overshadowed by Rebecca and getting her downstairs. He wanted it. And he knew that she would want it, too.

Alex frowned. "Brett, honestly, I still don't know why we're doing this."

"We've had run-ins with her for months now. I'm finishing it."

"And this has nothing to do with whatever you have going on with the CEO. This is too personal, and I don't like it. Listen, man, I respect you and your decisions, but I'm afraid you're not thinking with a clear head. Do you think it's the right thing? What if we just cut our losses, give up on this?"

"Are you fucking kidding me?" Brett looked, incredulous, at his friend. "Since when do we give up when something is a challenge?" He paused, reflecting on a question that he'd asked himself several times in the past couple of days. *Why don't we give up on this?* He blew out a heavy breath. "And besides, we can't stall the takeover now. How would that look to our own shareholders? It's too risky to appear weak." He shook his head. "I started this, and I own that. But we have to see it through. Our only option is to keep going and hope we can get Rebecca and RMD to back off."

Alex exhaled a deep breath, and he pushed his blond hair back. "Yeah."

Brett knew his friend wasn't convinced. "We've never been this divided on a move before, but trust me. This is going to work."

He hoped he was right.

CHAPTER TWELVE

REBECCA DIDN'T HAVE to check in with the doorman when she walked up the sidewalk. He moved aside to usher her in. "Good evening, Ms. Daniels."

She smiled and walked inside. Once she entered the now-familiar club, her head turned on a swivel, seeking out Brett's familiar figure in the crowd that mingled in the dimly lit room. And then she saw him. He was seated at a table with two men, no doubt members of The Brotherhood. He was talking, and what he said must have been funny, because the other two men burst out in deep laughter that vibrated off the walls of the club.

Brett smiled and took the opportunity to look away from his friends, and that was when his eyes locked with hers. All movement in the room stilled, the noise muted, and as they connected, he was the only thing that existed. After several beats, he turned back to his friends before standing and crossing the floor to meet her.

He looked devilishly handsome, dressed in a

black shirt, the sleeves rolled to the elbows, and black pants, and even though his smile was large, it didn't reach his eyes. When he was within reach, he extended his arm and grasped her hand in his, and he tugged her closer to him. His arms wrapped around her, lips dropping to hers, taking her in a breath-stealing kiss. Her lips parted under his and his tongue twined with hers as her arms wrapped around his neck, pulling her to him, not letting him get away.

When Rebecca thought she might pass out, she pulled away from him. "Hi," she whispered, her arms moving from his neck, lowering until her palms flattened against his chest, which rose and fell rapidly in time with her own.

He lowered his head and took her lips in another short, potent kiss. "Hey."

"Thank you for the flowers."

"Thank you for last night," he said as his lips turned upward. He smiled, but his face was unreadable. "And thank you for coming tonight."

Rebecca watched him for a moment, wondering briefly if he was angry at her, if he'd found out that she was RMD and a threat to his plan. But when he flattened his hands at her lower back, it no longer mattered. She allowed herself to melt against him, and once again, she found herself forgetting everything else that mattered to her, and she could focus only on him.

His palms dropped to her ass and he squeezed, and he let his large, knowing fingers dip lower, so that they reached the now-needy flesh of her pussy, which was already wet and ready for him. He stroked her through her dress until she moaned. And she didn't worry about the people all around them. No one was watching, and she leaned against him, wanting more, feeling his chuckle bubble from his chest.

A throat cleared behind them, and they pulled apart. She looked up and saw a man had appeared behind Brett. He looked nervous about interrupting them. "Um, Mr. Collins, everything is ready for you."

Brett smiled. "Thank you, Andre." The man turned away and left them alone again.

He extended his hand to her. "Come on."

"Where are we going?"

"You'll see."

Brett led Rebecca across the floor and down a staircase she hadn't noticed the last time she was here. He led her down a hallway and stopped at the first door. Brett opened it and moved aside to allow Rebecca to enter the room. It was a small square, and there was another door on the opposite wall. The room felt like a small vestibule.

"What's going on?"

"I've set something up for us, and I'm hoping you'll say yes."

That sounded cryptic to her, and she tilted her head to the side. "What is it?"

"You know how I told you earlier that we have some secrets downstairs? The things that only certain club members are invited to enjoy, no matter what their kink as long as it's between consenting adults?" He pointed to the other door. "On the other side of the door is one of our exhibition rooms."

"What do you mean?"

"You have an exhibitionist streak," he told her, and he opened the other door to the room. She peered around Brett's frame and saw it was small, with a bed in the center and glass panes for walls. He extended his hand to her and led her into the center of the room. "And you always have. The thrill of getting caught was something we both reveled in. But how about when we know people are watching us? I want to be with you here. In this room, in front of an audience. I think you'll like it."

Rebecca looked around the circular room and the curved, mirrored glass that covered the walls. "Brett, I don't know…"

He walked her farther into the room to stand by the bed. "This is a safe place to play out all of your fantasies. But there are a few other rooms if you're interested another time. We've got a professional dom and dominatrix on staff. We also have rooms set up for fire play, and some other things that people enjoy. But this room is for exhibition and voyeurism."

She turned around, putting her back to him, looking at the two-way mirrors, wondering if there were people watching them. "Brett, people will see."

"That's kind of the point, isn't it?"

"But what if they know us? They'll talk."

"They won't," he assured her. "Everyone who comes down here has to sign a confidentiality waiver. No one can discuss what happens here. No one will say anything."

"Are there people watching us now?" she asked, turning her head to look at him.

He nodded and stepped toward her. Standing behind her, he placed his palms on her shoulders. "The rooms are dark. They can see us, but we can't see them."

"How many people?" she asked, bringing her bottom lip between her teeth.

"There are eight private rooms in this area, surrounding this one. They can all see into this room, but we can't see them, nor can anyone see what's happening in any of the neighboring rooms, and I've been told that they're all occupied. And there's anywhere from two to five people in each room."

"Really?"

"Yeah," he answered, still behind her. He moved closer to her and pushed his hands down her front, over her chest. He palmed her breasts, through the satin of her dress. He leaned closer, and his lips brushed her ear. "Do you want to stay?"

Her entire body screamed in response to him, but she managed to quiet her shaky anticipation. "Yes," she whispered.

A shocked gasp passed through her parted lips when his hands grabbed her shoulders and turned her quickly to face him. "Well, we'd better give them one hell of show."

A slave to his desire, to Rebecca, Brett pulled her to him and kissed her. Sure, he'd brought her down here for ulterior motives. Bringing her down was a test. He wanted to seduce her, and then he would use her own desire against her, to get her to give up Daniels International, to give up and return to New York.

All of that was forgotten when his arms closed around her, pulling her small, lean body against his. She was warm, pliable, as his hands kneaded the muscles up and down the muscles of her back, until they grabbed her ass. She moaned and pressed closer, pushing herself into his dick. He'd already been hard when he met her upstairs, before he'd even touched her. His physiological reaction to Rebecca had always been immediate, almost desperate. He'd always blamed it on youthful eagerness, but at thirty, that enthusiasm for her hadn't waned.

He took a look around the room and knew that there were people on the other sides of the glass, watching them. He'd used the room before, but never with a woman like Rebecca. Those experiences didn't compare to his hands on Rebecca's body; and the minute she'd entered his life again, he knew he would take her down here. She had been the reason he'd insisted on the room in the first place.

He kissed her, remembering all of the times during college when they'd had sex in a public place. All over campus, under a blanket at Red Rock… even on an airplane once, heading off for spring break. Name a place, and he would probably be able to say that they'd had sex there. The risk of being caught was a thrill to both of them and had added to every encounter.

As his tongue plunged into her mouth, probing, stroking against hers, her fingers clenched, curling into the firm muscles of his chest, and she got to work unbuttoning his shirt. She pushed it off his shoulders, and he took less than a second to pull it from his wrists and discard it before he attacked her clothing with similar vigor. Their frantic actions took him off balance, and they both landed on the bed. It didn't manage to break their contact.

Sitting against the headboard, Brett pulled her into his lap, so her thighs straddled his hips. The short skirt of her satin shift dress rode up her parted thighs, and he could see that she hadn't worn any panties. He cupped her with his palm, delving a finger between her wet lips, finding her already wet. He spread her moisture around her clit, and she cried out in his mouth. "You skipped panties today?" he asked, his voice strained.

"Well, I knew that I would be seeing you, and despite our best intentions, we always seem to end up naked when we get together," she whispered. "Why waste time putting them on?"

He pulled his mouth away with a groan. "I like the way you think."

He grasped her waist, his fingers digging into her skin as he pulled her closer to him, pressing his hard cock into her bare pussy. She slid along his length. Her heat penetrated his pants, and he saw that she left a wet streak over the fly of his pants. The contact wasn't enough for either of them. The barrier of his pants, the way they restricted him, only frustrated him when all he wanted was to be inside her.

He released her mouth to trail kisses over her jaw, and then he dragged his teeth down her neck before sinking them into the delicate skin where it met her shoulder. Rebecca cried out in shock and pleasure, and she thrust her hips against him again.

He smoothed his palms over her bare ass and squeezed. He then pulled at the spaghetti straps of her dress and pulled down the material, uncovering her.

"This doesn't change anything between us, you know," she said to him as his lips descended on one of her nipples.

"What?" he asked, unsure how she was able to form any sort of sentence when all he could focus on was the taste of her skin.

"About how I'm not going to let you get your hands on my company?"

"Your company?" he breathed, before his teeth clamped lightly onto her left nipple, and she squealed as he pinched and played with the other with his fingers. "Remind me?" he said, his lips moving around her nipple to mutter the words. "I'm currently in the middle of acquiring a new firm, is that what you were talking about?"

She moaned as his mouth and fingers played her like a musical instrument. "Hmm… Yeah, I think you might be a little bit wrong about that. But I rather like where your hands are at the moment. So let's leave it for another time."

"Sounds good to me," he murmured against her stiff, needing nipple. "If you're able to think about anything else at the moment, then I must not be doing a good enough job." He flicked it with her tongue. She rubbed herself against him, leaving another spot of moisture on his pants. Her fingers dropped between them and unfastened his belt. She attacked his zipper with similar vigor. She put her hand in his boxers and withdrew his cock. He was hard, huge and ready. A drop of precum clung to the tip, and using her thumb, she spread the moisture over the head. His eyes were glued on her hands, and his lips parted. A breath shuddered from his chest. She shifted her hips, rubbing her wet pussy over the smooth skin of his length, sliding her wetness over him. She sighed at the contact, and she sped up the motion of her hips, but he didn't let himself enter her. He rubbed his member over her clit and watched her eyes roll back in pleasure.

Brett's fingers dug into the flesh of her ass, and he guided her hips over him, speeding up their rhythm even further. He groaned and let go of her briefly to reach into his pocket. He pulled out a condom. "Stop, Becca. Any more and I'll come."

He moved away from her, long enough to remove his pants. He discarded them where they fell on the floor and quickly returned to her on the bed.

Rebecca took the condom from his fingers and ripped open the foil packet. She covered him with the latex and held him in her fist, while she lowered herself over him, impaling herself on him until she was fully seated in his lap.

The sensation of her was always overwhelming, she was so warm and welcoming. She took a deep breath, clenched around him, tightening, and he groaned. She didn't move. He briefly thought about the people watching them, and how they were there for an erotic show. But Brett didn't care. He would stay there with Rebecca seated on his dick forever. The firmness of the mattress and her weight in his lap kept him in place. He tried to pull his hips back, to begin, but she was in full control. He exhaled a frustrated breath. "Christ, move," he pleaded.

With a small smile on her lips, she kissed him chastely on the lips. But she obliged him and lifted herself over him, swiveling her hips, drawing out of him and then plunging down again. The desperate, growing ache within him needed it to be faster, harder. His hands gripped her hips, aiding her movements again, digging into her flesh.

"You're so goddamn sexy, Rebecca. Just keep riding my dick. Just like that. Fuck," he said, his lips brushing against the skin of her chest. Her breasts bounced with each thrust, and when he realized that she was completely on display, something snapped within Brett. He didn't want the guests on the other side of the reflective glass to see her. Rebecca was his, and he didn't want anyone else to enjoy her.

But there was no way in hell he would stop. Nothing short of death could interrupt him while he made love to her. In one quick movement, he rolled them both over, so she was on her back, and he covered her body. He took control and continued to plunge into her. She gripped his back, digging in with her nails, and the pain mixed with pleasure was a sweet dichotomy that caused a stirring low in his belly, that radiated throughout him. She cried out in his ear and she came, and he felt her contractions around his cock. It was enough to bring him over the edge, as well. He came, his cock buried deep inside her, with his own hoarse shout.

He caught his breath, and even though he knew that he might have been crushing her, he couldn't find the energy or the will to move. He wanted to stay with her for the rest of the evening. He knew he couldn't, but he wasn't sure if he could make it back up the stairs without constant physical contact with her.

He realized that he had to get rid of the condom, and he reluctantly disengaged from her and dropped the spent latex in the nearby garbage. She lay back on the bed, her breasts exposed to him, and he reached out again and touched her. His eyes were heavy, his bones liquid, but his skin was electric, sensitized. He grabbed his pants and pulled them on. He held out his hand to her. "Come on."

"Where are we going?"

"I'm going to take you home," he told her. "We're going to bed."

CHAPTER THIRTEEN

BRETT WOKE WITH a groan and rolled over, not at first recognizing where he was. It took a moment to acclimate to the strange surroundings, and he remembered that he was in Rebecca's bed. They'd gone there, arms wrapped around each other, kissing all the way from her front door until they reached her bed, where they collapsed and he took her again before they fell asleep, their limbs entangled.

He felt Rebecca's warmth next to him, and he reached out and smoothed his palm over her lush curves. She moaned in her sleep and turned to face him. The thin sheet that covered her shifted, revealing her perfect breasts. He'd gone to bed with her. It had been a long time since he'd actually *slept* with a woman, sharing the same bed. After sex, he normally vacated the premises as quickly as possible, not wanting to stick around for the messy conversations and expectations that often came along with spending the night.

He watched Rebecca sleep in the moonlight. The

delicate rise and fall of her chest entranced him, and he wanted to wake her, just so he could take her again, plunge into her naked, waiting body. But he didn't. Instead, he smiled and pulled her closer, and he let himself feel a comfort he hadn't felt before. In five years, so much had changed, but it felt like nothing had at all. Rebecca stirred in her sleep and she snuggled closer, placing her head on his chest. He placed a tender kiss on the top of her head and lay back down.

He could have loved her. Probably. If their past wasn't so complicated, and if they weren't currently embroiled in a corporate feud. But he furrowed his brow. It couldn't be love. He'd never loved any woman. And he couldn't have been in love with Rebecca. It wasn't possible.

The light they'd left on in the hallway shone in through the door they'd left open, and it was in his eyes. Brett pushed himself out of bed to go turn it off. He walked naked into the hallway and saw the switch a little farther down. With his hand on the plastic lever, he noticed that he was standing outside her office. From his spot in the hallway, he saw the discarded coffee mug and papers strewed over the top of the desk, and there was even a bra thrown in the corner. He laughed, imagining her coming home from work and going straight to her home office to do more work, taking off her bra to get comfortable.

He took a quick look at the door to her bedroom, where Rebecca still slept. He took a step into the darkened office. He turned on her desk lamp and scanned through a stack on top, and he choked on his breath when he saw the letterhead—*RMD Holdings*. "Fuck me," Brett whispered, and it hit him. "RMD. Rebecca Madeline Daniels." *The holdings company is named with her goddamn initials.* He looked over the documents and saw records of the transactions of her stock acquisitions. He shook his head. He couldn't believe he hadn't made the connection before.

"See anything interesting?"

He whipped around and saw her standing in the door. "Yeah, I did." He gestured to her with the paper. "You're RMD?"

"And if I am?"

"You're buying shares of Daniels International, as well?"

"Yes. It's a power move. To save my company."

"That's interesting."

"What are you doing in my office?" she asked, walking toward him.

He shrugged. "I had to make a phone call and I couldn't find my cell phone," he lied easily. "I looked down and saw your letterhead. So you're buying out your own company."

"Of course. It's not ideal, but I won't let you take my company from me."

"Why couldn't we find any information on what RMD is?"

"You had me investigated?"

"Yes," he said, unflinching. "We had to know what we were up against in our takeover bid."

"My father gave me shares when I left town, but he didn't want anyone to know they were mine. I guess he thought I wouldn't be able to protect my own stake in the company when he was gone. He didn't want me vulnerable. So he created the holding company for me. Nobody knows it's me. I think it was his way of keeping controlling interest away from others. He never imagined that I could take care of it myself. He should have known better."

Brett frowned. He understood her father's intentions, but while Rebecca might be a lot of things, *vulnerable* certainly wasn't one of them. But something else she'd said nagged at him.

He had an idea, a way that they could both survive, and that he could save face. "This is great. Why don't you sign your shares over to Alex and me? You can work for us. We'll give you a great executive position at Collins/Fischer."

Her eyes widened, and she gave a short, loud guffaw. "You're out of your goddamn mind. I didn't work this hard to sign over my rightful property to you."

"Hear me out. DI has been struggling for years. An acquisition by my company can keep the company from folding completely. The shareholders are happy. You can come work for me. Everyone will get what they want."

"Not me," she said. "That isn't what I want. I'm going to rise and restore Daniels International to the great company it was. No matter what it takes. I don't need your help. I have my own plans, and I will never sell out my father's company." She took a deep breath. "You should leave."

"Rebecca—"

"Get out!"

Brett blew out a frustrated breath. "Fine. I'll go," he said, stalking past her. "Goddammit," he muttered. "But mark my words. We're not done here. I'll see you Friday at the shareholders' meeting, and don't think for a second that any of the holdouts are going to stick with you over me."

Brett slammed his fist on the steering wheel as he pulled his car out onto the road. He didn't know if he was madder at her or himself. He knew he couldn't be angry at her for trying to protect her family business. That last remark was his lashing out, probably unfairly, and he settled his anger on himself. How had he let the fact that Rebecca was behind RMD get by him? *Goddammit*, he knew exactly how. He'd been distracted. If only he hadn't been so caught up in his own life, in her and her body. He should have been smarter, more aware.

She'd vowed to stop them. Did that include using him, keeping him close to stop him?

Using the car's Bluetooth system, he called Alex. After several rings, his friend answered, out of breath. "Dude, do you have any idea what time it is?" he said by way of greeting. "I'm not exactly alone here."

"It's Rebecca," Brett said.

"What's Rebecca?"

"RMD. It's her fucking initials." Brett quickly explained what had gone down in Rebecca's office.

Alex was quiet for a bit. "Are you kidding?"

"I wish I was. Her dad set up the holding company in secret years ago. She bought up all those shares in the last week using her own money."

"Well, shit," Alex breathed out.

"Alex..." Brett heard an annoyed, disembodied female voice in the background. Alex's late-night company.

"Dude, let's get together tomorrow morning," Brett said. "We've got to get our shit together before the stockholders' meeting on Friday. Get back to your night."

CHAPTER FOURTEEN

REBECCA TAPPED HER fingers impatiently on her desk. A nervous, angry energy ran through her. She tried focusing on work but to no avail. The words and numbers on the computer screen in front of her blurred. She was mad. Mad at Brett, mad at herself.

She hadn't seen Brett in several days, not since he'd found out she was RMD. She knew that his ego had prevented him from reaching out to her. To be honest, her ego had caused the same. He was a proud man, and the fact that she'd bested him had made him angry. But that didn't dull the ache, the hollow, in her chest. The short time that Brett had been in her life had affected her more than she'd ever imagined it could. It hurt to think about, so every time she'd thought about him, she'd doubled her efforts into saving Daniels International.

But there was something about Brett. He did something to her. And Rebecca wondered if another man had ever made her feel the way Brett did. She'd never been in love. Was that what she was feeling? Was it possible that she was actually in love with Brett Collins?

"No!" she told herself, her voice firm and strong in her empty office.

But are you sure?

No! Brett was everything she hated—privilege, arrogance, stubbornness. But goddammit, he was sexy, fun, adventurous, and they were able to relate on a level that she'd never experienced with another man. She clenched her fists. It was lust, not love. He was gorgeous and incredible in bed, but that didn't mean anything. There were millions of good-looking guys in the world. She'd never met one as good in bed as Brett was, but that didn't mean anything. He was just one man among millions.

But Rebecca couldn't ignore the way her heartbeat increased speed, how her breath became shallow. Maybe it was love. She shook herself free of it. She couldn't be in love with Brett. They were similar in nature, sexually compatible, but they were also enemies. She had no future with him.

She frowned and checked her watch. The shareholders' meeting would start in ten minutes, and she would face down Brett, Alex and the other few shareholders who remained. She stood and tried to mentally psyche herself up for what would probably be an epic showdown. She'd worked hard, but there was one more step, and that would be appealing to the last few remaining holdouts—then she would own more than enough to secure sole ownership of the business. It was time, so she gathered her things and headed upstairs.

When she got to the conference room, she saw that she was the first one there, except for the catering team who were busy putting together a coffee station and trays of fruit and pastries. They offered her a cup of coffee, which she gratefully accepted, and she took a seat at the head of the table.

Slowly, each seat of the table became occupied by the holdouts, the older men who had known her father, and as the meeting start time drew closer, there were still two unoccupied seats—Brett's and Alex's.

She checked her watch again. It was ten on the dot. Time to start. If Brett didn't want to show, she would just go ahead and start without him. Standing, she smiled at those in attendance. Between the push for shares by Brett and herself, the number of shareholders in the room had dwindled greatly.

"Gentlemen," she addressed them. "Thank you for coming today. Now, looking around the room, there are far fewer of us than there was the last time we all met."

The door opened, interrupting her. She looked and saw Brett and Alex enter the room. They walked to the table and sat as if they owned the place. Hell, they probably thought that they did. But it wasn't over yet.

"Sorry we're late," Brett said, sitting back comfortably in his chair.

"The meeting started at ten," she reminded him.

"Yes, forgive us for our tardiness," Brett said, extending his hand. "Please continue."

Rebecca then turned back to the rest of the men. "Gentlemen, I thank you for your patience, but I've gathered you here today because I know you all. I know that you were all close to my father. And out of that loyalty to him, you were reluctant to sell your shares to the two companies that approached you to sell. I want to thank you for that." She tried to catch the eye of each man in the room, to let them know her thanks was heartfelt.

"This is my first shareholders' meeting since I became CEO, and I know if my father were here at this meeting, he would start by talking about Daniels International's profits and future plans, but I need to address the elephant in the room." Rebecca cast a glance at Brett. "When Collins/Fischer sent a tender offer on our company, many people sold their shares for the premium they were paying. You didn't. And to secure the rest of the company, RMD stepped up to stop them from taking over. And you still held on. But I want to tell you that RMD is me, and to my father's memory, I am standing up to the cannibalization of real estate development in Las Vegas. Collins/Fischer's goal is to be the only name in real estate in this town. But we can't let that happen. A monopoly would be good for no one."

"If I may interrupt for a second." Brett's deep voice rang out in the room. Rebecca looked up and saw that Brett was now standing, a grim smile turning his lips upward. "Sorry, gentlemen, *ma'am*." He acknowledged her, the only woman in the room, with a brief nod. Her eyes locked on his for a brief moment. At that moment, he wasn't her larger-than-life lover. He was cold, methodical. This was Brett Collins in business mode.

"What do you want?" she asked.

He seemed amused that she was the only one to speak up, and one corner of his mouth ticked upward. "Well, we wanted to take advantage of all of the remaining shareholders in the room. By now, we know you've all received our letters and know our intent." Brett glanced around the room. "We're shareholders in Daniels International. We have just as much reason to be here as anyone else does."

"Nobody else in this room is in the middle of a hostile takeover of the company," Rebecca told him.

He ignored her and turned to the rest of the men in the room. "Gentlemen, what we're doing here today is to talk to you about selling your shares in DI. You've seen our offer, and you've seen Ms. Daniels's offer. But let's be blunt. Daniels International has seen a steady decline in profits in the past decade, and the value of your shares is going down. We're now offering an even higher premium for your shares. If you're interested in selling, we're now offering more than fifty percent above the market value." Eyes widened as they named their new price, including Rebecca's, and she seethed at the gall of the man. To come into her meeting and begin complete destruction of the business that she was trying to protect...

Putting her palms on the table, Rebecca looked around the room. "Gentlemen, please," she started. "I know what Mr. Collins and Mr. Fischer are offering is very generous, but it's foolhardy. Daniels International is on the way back up, I promise. We have big plans for the future, which I will gladly detail once Mr. Collins sits down. Have profits been declining? Sure. There's no question of that. But we're going to make a big comeback, and you don't want this to be the way you give up your stake in this great company. You all knew my father and saw this company in its heyday," she said. "We're going to bring this company back to where it was, and we'll be better than ever. You have my word."

She felt Brett's glare on her, but she ignored him, basking in the agreement of several of the men in the room, all old friends of her father's. They'd held on to her every word, nodding in alliance as she detailed Daniels International's plans for the future. She cast a defiant look at Brett, still standing on the other side of the table, his mouth open,

poised to speak over her, but she looked at him in
challenge and was surprised to see him back down.

She raised an eyebrow and then addressed the
room. "I think that's everything today, gentlemen.
Meeting adjourned." Without another look at Brett,
Rebecca gathered her belongings and was the first
to leave the room.

CHAPTER FIFTEEN

BRETT LEANED HIS elbows on the bar at Di Terrestres.
The club was full, but no one bothered him; it must
have been obvious he wasn't in the mood to be approached. He was pissed. Frustrated. He wanted to
grab a bottle of five-hundred-dollar bourbon from
behind the bar and go up to his office and polish
the thing off. But he didn't. Like most people who
grappled with addiction, his sobriety was a daily
struggle, and he normally had tighter grip on it.
The stubbornness to not go back to "old Brett" was
what allowed him to own a bar. But some days were
harder than others. And it had been a hard day.
He stayed at the bar, where there were witnesses,
people to whom he was accountable. He clenched
his fists in wanting. Things had not gone the way
they were planned.

Rebecca was staying put, and he'd have to deal
with her being a regular presence in the local real
estate industry. It was his problem, not hers, and he
never should have dragged her into it. He thought

he'd owned the world, could do anything he wanted, but in one fell swoop, he'd lost it all. Because of his stupid, foolish pride, he'd lost out on a business goal that had not only cost him money but was a blow to his reputation. No one else in the boardroom had agreed to sell to him, no matter what he'd said. The remaining shareholders were all loyal to the company and the Daniels name. And his scheming had also cost him the only woman he'd ever cared about.

He grimaced. He thought he could have loved Rebecca. But it would never work between them. There was too much bad blood and animosity, especially now that he'd tried to take her company from her. She'd played her part, but he was the one who'd sounded the death knell for any relationship they could have had. He'd ruined everything.

"I should have known we'd find you here," he heard Rafael say from behind him. Alex was with him, and they joined him at the bar, flanking him. "We tried calling you."

"Yeah, my phone's off."

His friends eyed his glass warily.

"It's water."

"What's going on?" Rafael asked.

He shook his head. "Did you ever feel like you just ruined everything?"

"No, but I generally do everything right," Rafael answered.

The bartender came over with drinks for Alex

and Rafael and then left quickly, knowing that they were engaged in serious conversation. Brett turned to Alex. "I'm sorry."

"What about?"

"I'm sorry I got us involved in a venture we couldn't win. It was my pride that was motivating me. And we lost."

"It's fine," Alex said, even though Brett knew that Alex was just as upset as he was. "Just be straight with me from now on."

"I will," he promised.

"Seriously, though. Why are you moping? We've lost deals and takeover bids before." Alex stopped. "It's just business. We'll get the next one." He paused. "You can admit it, you know. This was all about Rebecca, wasn't it? Are you in love with her?"

He nodded. "She fucking hates me."

"Yeah, probably."

"I guess the party's here," someone else called from behind him. When the three of them turned, they saw Alana and Gabe join them at the bar. Alana went behind the bar, dodging the busy bartenders, and she grabbed an unopened bottle of wine and a bottle of Perrier for Brett, and the group moved on to their regular table. "What's with the long faces? I take it the Daniels International shareholders' meeting didn't exactly go as planned?"

Brett guffawed. "You got that right." He filled

them in on the details of the meeting. "Needless to say, our takeover bid of Daniels is over."

"Good for her!" Alana exclaimed, her smile wide. "That's fantastic!"

"Not for us," Alex groused.

"I'm sorry it's not want you wanted, but I'm so proud of her. She was alone and worked her ass off to save her company. You have to respect that."

"Alana's right. You've got to give it to Rebecca. She's one hell of a businesswoman," Rafael reasoned.

"So she beat you. Is that why you're sulking?" Alana asked.

"I'm not sulking," Brett snapped.

Alana poured herself a glass of wine and raised it. "Here's to Rebecca. It's nice to see a woman come out on top in this city sometimes."

Brett raised his glass and clinked it against hers. He couldn't fault Rebecca. She was going to be good for Daniels International, and if anyone could restore it to its former glory, it was her.

"Shall she always be a thorn in Brett Collins's side," Gabe finished. "So, are you guys going to hold on to the Daniels stocks or what?"

"We'll have to come up with some sort of plan. I don't know. I fucked up with her. I need to make it right."

"Dude, you have my blessing to do whatever you need to do," Alex said.

Brett nodded. Despite that he'd hurt Rebecca, he was happy for her. Proud of her success. He'd given her a run for her money and she'd come out on top—it was admirable.

Brett was grateful to still have his friend's trust. "Thanks for everything, guys." He stood and walked away. Even though they were trying to talk business and joke around with him, he couldn't handle their concerned looks. He needed some time alone.

He didn't realize that Alana had followed him. "You love her, don't you?" she asked.

He didn't say anything for a while as he dwelled on the time he'd spent with her. She was gorgeous, sexy, but tough. He respected her, and she took up way too much of his mind, and he could only think about when he would be able to see her again. Somehow, somewhere along the way, he *had* fallen in love with her. Brett nodded. "Yeah, I think I do." Rebecca had been right. If he'd set all of this aside, he could've spent the last few weeks focusing on things that really mattered, instead of blindly trying to shut her down. Only now did he realize what he'd lost.

He'd been stupid, pigheaded, and he owed her an apology. He laughed to himself. For a man who apologized to no one for anything, a man who took what he wanted, who only thought of himself, he only ever found himself apologizing to Rebecca Daniels.

"So, what are you going to do to make it right?"

"I don't know. I need some grand gesture, don't I?"

"Probably. Let me know how it goes," she said, patting him on the shoulder before she walked back to the table.

On Monday morning, Rebecca spun around in her chair. The view of the mountains made her smile, and it was one of things she missed every minute she'd been in New York. But for the first time since she'd returned to her home city, she felt lighter, like a weight had been lifted from her shoulders. She turned around and looked around her newly redesigned office. She'd made the space hers—feminine, modern, friendly—and it finally felt like she was coming into her own in the role of CEO. She was the boss and not just her father's replacement.

Now it came time to work. It would be hard to turn the company around, and she was still on shaky ground. It had been tough, all the work, the turmoil it had caused her personal life, but nevertheless she'd persisted.

And it had paid off. She alone was the majority shareholder of Daniels International, and while Collins/Fischer still owned a fair amount of shares, they could do nothing. She'd held them off. Daniels International was safe from their grasp.

She studied the folders in front of her. She had a lot of work to do to pull Daniels International back to its former state of prestige, as she'd promised the remaining few shareholders. And she knew that it would be an uphill battle for her. But at least things were looking up for her and the company, and she'd done the right thing for herself, the people who worked there and her father's legacy, even if it cost her the man she loved.

Love? The word had surprised her as it popped up in her mind. Rebecca wasn't sure when her feelings about Brett had transitioned from contempt to like to love. How could she love him? He'd tried to ruin her. But in the process, he'd made her work even harder. Brett consumed her, and he always had. No matter what her brain told her, the reasons she shouldn't be with him, she couldn't quiet the uncontrollable quiver in her chest when she thought of him. But no matter when it had happened, and what her thoughts about him were, it was over.

"You said goodbye to him once," she told herself. "You can do it again."

Amy buzzed in on the intercom, interrupting her introspection. "Brett Collins is here to see you."

Her eyes widened in shock. He was the last person she'd expected to see. "Send him in."

The door opened and he walked in. "Hi," he said.

He looked at her desk, which she'd covered with documents. "Catching up on work?"

"Yeah, we've got a lot of things to do to bring Daniels International back to the top. What can I help you with? Why are you here?"

He blew out a heavy sigh, and he looked around the room before his eyes met hers again. "Because I was an ass."

"Really?" She rolled her eyes. "You? An ass? That doesn't sound like you at all."

"I deserve that."

She nodded. "You do."

"I'm sorry for what happened between us. And I'm mostly sorry for trying to take over your company."

She cocked her head to the side and smiled somewhat mirthlessly. "What is it? Are you here to tell me that you want some big-businessman tips? I can be your mentor, help you out if you want some coaching."

He grinned but sobered. "Seriously. I shouldn't have done it. I'm sorry," he said. "For everything."

She nodded.

"I don't really know how we got here."

She had no response to that—she knew Brett had always been competitive, but he'd bordered on ruthless these last few weeks. Still, she hadn't expected him to come down here and apologize. That seemed out of character for him. "And maybe I'm a little sore because I didn't get everything I wanted," Brett said softly. "I usually do."

"You can take over other businesses, you know. Just leave mine alone."

"It has nothing to do with business." He pulled an envelope from the inside pocket of his coat, put it on the desk between them and slid it over to her.

"What's this?"

"A letter. We drew it up this morning. The shares that Alex and I held in Daniels International, we want to transfer them back to you."

"Brett. What—"

"We don't need them. We don't want them. You deserve them, and now you'll never lose control of your family firm again."

"But why?"

Brett took a deep breath and looked at the floor for a moment before his eyes found hers. "I don't give a damn about business, making deals, mergers, acquisitions. I just want you."

Her mouth dropped, and he stood and came around to her side of the desk. He reached down, took her hands and pulled her up so that she was standing. "What do you mean?" she asked.

"I want you. And I'll do anything to have you."

"Brett—"

"I love you," he said quickly.

Rebecca watched him. And he raised a hand to push through his hair. She wanted to hold him, the longing tearing through her chest. "What?" She wasn't sure she'd heard the words that he'd said to her and needed confirmation.

"Rebecca, I love you," he repeated. "I've never loved anyone before, and I don't know when it happened or how. But I know that I've been miserable without you."

Brett's declaration caused some tears to pool at the corners of her eyes. She blinked them away and put down the letter. "Brett, I love you, too."

"Do you think we can? Can we be happy together?"

"If we're always honest and put each other first over the job, I think we can try."

He put his hands on either side of her face and pulled her toward him. He kissed her deeply, and her knees buckled in relief from his touch, but as long as he was holding her, she wouldn't fall.

She pulled back and took another look at the stacks of files on her table.

"What? Do you need to get back to work?" he asked her. His lips brushed against hers.

"No," she said. "I think I can put it off until tomorrow."

"Good," he said and, with a swipe of his arm, he brushed all the stacks of folders on the floor and then lifted her onto the desk.

Her dress had ridden up her hips, and he reached for her panties. She lifted her hips, and he removed the satin barrier. He undid his zipper and lowered his pants. She held her breath as he withdrew his cock from his pants and slowly stepped toward her. He withdrew a condom from the front pocket of his pants and covered himself.

He palmed her and he dipped his thumb between her wet folds, tracing the lines of her pussy. He circled the bundle of nerves of her clit and Rebecca moaned and bucked her hips. She cried out, perhaps a little too loudly, and she briefly wondered if Amy could hear her outside the thick doors of the office. "Brett, do it now," she pleaded. She needed to feel him again. She was desperate, crying out for his attention.

He held himself over her, and he placed the tip of his cock against her wet folds and pushed inside her, hard and deep. He leaned over and braced himself with a palm on the desk next to her, and he pulled back his hips and plunged into her again. His pace was quick and forceful.

The only sounds in the room were his grunts, her gasps and the sound of his thighs slapping against the inside of hers. She knew she wouldn't last much longer. He buried his face in the crook of her neck and kissed and licked the sensitive skin before nipping her shoulder between his teeth. It was enough for her. Her quick breathing turned to lustful screams as she called out. Then he shook as he grunted out with his own release.

He lay over her for more several moments, unable to move or speak, and Rebecca concentrated on just trying to regain her breath.

Brett supported his weight on his strong forearms. "I must be crushing you," he whispered, his breath heavy and warm against her ear.

"No, it's nice," she told him.

With a moan, he pushed himself upward. He was somehow still hard inside her, and the movement shifted his position inside her. The noise she made was a mixture of pleasure from stimulation and missing the warmth of his body on top of hers.

He smiled down at her. "Sorry, I've got to get rid of this condom." He strode into the kitchen and reappeared after a moment.

"Did you bring that just assuming that I would forgive you and we'd have sex?"

He shrugged and grinned slowly. "I didn't know for sure, but you can't blame a guy for hoping." He pulled on his pants and, forgetting his shirt, stooped to pick up the papers that were strewed over the floor. "Sorry about the mess."

Rebecca pushed herself up on her elbows. "It's okay. It was time to stop for the day anyway." She looked down and saw that Brett was sitting in the middle of the floor, amid the mess of papers, wearing a goofy grin on his face. He looked up at her.

"What's so funny?" she asked him.

He stood. "It's amazing. That we're both here

right now. I spent every day of the last five years trying not to remember you, but I couldn't not want you. I never thought I would get another chance. And then I finally did, and I screwed it up again. I really did miss you."

"I missed you, too. But let's not screw it up this time, all right? And let's leave the work at the office from now on. No more lies, no more business interfering with our relationship."

He stuck out his right hand and she shook it. "Deal."

* * * * *

LET'S TALK
Romance

For exclusive extracts, competitions
and special offers, find us online:

f facebook.com/millsandboon

⦿ @millsandboonuk

🐦 @millsandboon

Or get in touch on 0844 844 1351*

For all the latest titles coming soon, visit
millsandboon.co.uk/nextmonth

Calls cost 7p per minute plus your phone company's price per minute access charge